SECOND CHANCES

"Having a guy like you is only the first step," Rusty explained to Joanne. "You've got to keep his interest and make it grow. I can think of a million relationships that fizzled out before they even got started."

"A million?" Joanne asked skeptically.

"Well, half a million." Rusty laughed. "But I think you've got a point about Tony maybe liking more sophisticated girls. After all, his brother dates Skye, and you know how together she is. She's probably a role model for him—for what a girl should be."

"You mean you think he'd like me better if I was more like Skye?"

"Exactly," Rusty replied.

"Then I'm sunk. I'll never be as sophisticated as she is."

"Sure you will. All you need is a new wardrobe, a crash course in popular culture, and a whole lot of practice."

Bantam Sweet Dreams Romances
Ask your bookseller for the books you have missed

#1	P.S. I LOVE YOU	#54	I CAN'T FORGET YOU
#2	THE POPULARITY PLAN	#55	SPOTLIGHT ON LOVE
#3	LAURIE'S SONG	#56	CAMPFIRE NIGHTS
#4	PRINCESS AMY	#57	ON HER OWN
#5	LITTLE SISTER	#58	RHYTHM OF LOVE
#6	CALIFORNIA GIRL	#59	PLEASE SAY YES
#7	GREEN EYES	#60	SUMMER BREEZES
#8	THE THOROUGHBRED	#61	EXCHANGE OF HEARTS
#9	COVER GIRL	#62	JUST LIKE THE MOVIES
#10	LOVE MATCH	#63	KISS ME, CREEP
#11	THE PROBLEM WITH LOVE	#64	LOVE IN THE FAST LANE
#12	NIGHT OF THE PROM	#65	THE TWO OF US
#13	THE SUMMER JENNY FELL IN LOVE	#66	LOVE TIMES TWO
#14	DANCE OF LOVE	#67	I BELIEVE IN YOU
#15	THINKING OF YOU	#68	LOVEBIRDS
#16	HOW DO YOU SAY GOODBYE	#69	CALL ME BEAUTIFUL
#17	ASK ANNIE	#70	SPECIAL SOMEONE
#18	TEN-BOY SUMMER	#71	TOO MANY BOYS
#19	LOVE SONG	#72	GOODBYE FOREVER
#20	THE POPULARITY SUMMER	#73	LANGUAGE OF LOVE
#22	SECRET IDENTITY	#74	DON'T FORGET ME
#23	FALLING IN LOVE AGAIN	#75	FIRST SUMMER LOVE
#24	THE TROUBLE WITH CHARLIE	#76	THREE CHEERS FOR LOVE
#26	IT MUST BE MAGIC	#77	TEN-SPEED SUMMER
#27	TOO YOUNG FOR LOVE	#78	NEVER SAY NO
#29	NEVER LOVE A COWBOY	#79	STAR STRUCK!
#30	LITTLE WHITE LIES	#80	A SHOT AT LOVE
#32	DAYDREAMER	#81	SECRET ADMIRER
#35	FORBIDDEN LOVE	#82	HEY, GOOD LOOKING!
#36	SUMMER DREAMS	#83	LOVE BY THE BOOK
#38	RUNNING MATES	#84	THE LAST WORD
#39	FIRST LOVE	#85	THE BOY SHE LEFT BEHIND
#40	SECRETS	#86	QUESTIONS OF LOVE
#41	THE TRUTH ABOUT ME & BOBBY V.	#87	PROGRAMMED FOR LOVE
		#88	WRONG KIND OF BOY
#45	DREAM PROM	#89	101 WAYS TO MEET MR. RIGHT
#47	TE AMO MEANS I LOVE YOU	#90	TWO'S A CROWD
#48	DIAL L FOR LOVE	#91	THE LOVE HUNT
#49	TOO MUCH TO LOSE	#92	KISS AND TELL
#50	LIGHTS, CAMERA, LOVE	#93	THE GREAT BOY CHASE
#53	GHOST OF A CHANCE	#94	SECOND CHANCES

Second Chances

Nancy Levinson

BANTAM BOOKS
TORONTO • NEW YORK • LONDON • SYDNEY • AUCKLAND

RL 5, IL age 11 and up

SECOND CHANCES
A Bantam Book / September 1985

Cover photo by Pat Hill

ISBN 0-553-25132-5

Published simultaneously in the United States and Canada

PRINTED IN THE UNITED STATES OF AMERICA

O   0 9 8 7 6 5 4 3 2 1

Second Chances

Chapter One

This is it, Joanne Trask thought as she settled comfortably into her airplane seat. *I'm finally on my way.* She pushed a few reddish-brown strands of hair out of her eyes and looked eagerly out the window. *My first time on an airplane; my first time outside Alaska; my first school with a real art teacher!* she thought excitedly, a little tingle running up her spine.

Slowly the airplane rolled forward, then accelerated down the runway. It sped faster until it lifted smoothly off the ground. *Hey,* Joanne said to herself, *I'm really flying!*

She watched the airport below grow smaller and smaller until the cars looked like scurrying bugs and the homes in the town below resembled the plastic houses of a Monopoly game. As the airplane climbed higher, even these became too small to pick out clearly.

Joanne promised herself she'd do a drawing of Alaska when she got her feet back on the ground again. Everything looked so different up there, seen through a veil of misty, white clouds. *Well*, she thought, *I'd better get used to things being different. Everything's going to be very different when I get to California.*

California! Joanne had friends who had visited there, and they'd said it was really something else. One girl had said it felt like being on another planet. And very possibly she was right. There probably weren't two places that contrasted more than Joanne's hometown, the tiny, tucked-away village of Scranton, Alaska, and the fashionable, modern suburb of Los Angeles where she was headed.

To Joanne, California was a place where flowers bloomed all year round and where a lot of really sophisticated kids lived. She'd read about those kids in magazine articles and seen them on TV talent shows. Now she was actually going to meet them, to go to school with them. Her grandparents said that kids in the California suburb of New Falls always had something to do. After living in the sleepy town of Scranton for so many years, Joanne was eager to do everything—twice!

She looked at her reflection in the window of the plane, then smiled widely at her own image. Her blue eyes sparkled above high, freckled cheekbones, and her skin was clear and peach-colored from the sun. Her expression was open and friendly. She reached up again to push those few stray hairs out of her face. They had escaped from the single thick braid that reached just past her shoulder blades. Joanne tucked her long legs underneath her and smiled again as if she alone knew some wonderful secret.

"Excuse me, is this your first trip on an airplane?"

Joanne turned to find her seatmate, a grandmotherly woman with big round glasses and white hair, gazing at her curiously. "Um, yes, it is," Joanne said. "How did you know?"

"Well, you look so—so enthusiastic," the woman replied kindly.

"You bet I'm enthusiastic," Joanne answered. "This is the biggest adventure of my life. I've never even been outside Alaska. I've lived my whole life, sixteen years, in Scranton. And now I'm going to spend an entire year living with my grandparents in California."

"How nice," the woman said, smiling. "Where do they live?"

"In a town called New Falls," Joanne replied.

"Oh, I've been there. It's a lovely place. The

scenery is beautiful, and there's so much going on there. They have a cute little theater and two art museums."

Joanne flashed her seatmate a quick grin. "I've heard about those museums," she told the older woman. "See, the main reason I'm going to live with my grandparents is that New Falls High has such a great art program. I want to get some good training and build up my portfolio so that I have a better chance when I apply to art schools next year."

"I must say, you're very brave," the woman said.

Joanne smiled. "I feel a little as if I'm standing on the high diving board at the swimming pool. I guess that by getting on this plane, I've already taken the jump. I mean, there's no going back now."

As Joanne said those words, she felt a little twinge of fear shoot down to the pit of her stomach. There really wasn't any way to back out of the trip at this point. She had already said goodbye to her family, her home, and her friends. Now, she was about to say hello to who knew what!

Joanne thought about her last walk through Scranton, which she'd taken that afternoon. She had looked around carefully, as if she were trying to memorize every detail of the little town.

Of course, after living for sixteen years in a place as small as Scranton, she already knew details like who lived in which house, what they did, and what they were like. But it was the fresh, sharp smell of the air she had concentrated on, the clear brightness of the high, expansive sky, and the exact color of the tiny tundra flowers.

Joanne pictured Scranton again clearly in her mind. There was Main Street, just a strip of blacktop without any sidewalks or streetlights. Actually, it was pretty misleading to call it Main Street. It wasn't the town's main street; it was its *only* street. Usually after school the younger kids would roller-skate up and down that long, smooth strip of blacktop. Of course, they didn't have the fancy skates Joanne had seen on TV commercials; their metal skates simply clamped onto their sneakers. Betsey, David, and Ellen were out almost every day.

Those kids were younger than Joanne, but she loved them just the same. In Scranton everyone knew everyone. Joanne had grown up playing with kids of all ages. There weren't enough people around to be choosy about how old your friends were. She couldn't imagine going to a school with five hundred kids in her own grade. That was more than the whole population of Scranton!

Thinking about New Falls High made Joanne

nervous. She wondered if she'd really be able to fit in with all those sophisticated L.A. suburban kids. *You shouldn't worry*, she told herself firmly. *You'll still be the same person when you get to L.A., and you like yourself just fine right now.*

She pushed her doubts from her mind and went back to picturing Scranton. She could see the brightly painted wooden houses that stood on either side of Main Street. The pink, green, and blue buildings added a little color to the town in winter, when the trees were bare and everything was covered with snow. The houses were always well cared for and well loved, but they were nothing fancy, each one a variation on the same simple box design. Like everything up north, they were built to be sturdy, usable, and lasting, not decorative or luxurious.

Joanne thought lovingly of her own blue house with its neat white trim. She had always felt so warm and secure in it, even during the most severe winter storms. Her best friend, Maya, lived next door to her. Then came old Mrs. Barstein and her cat. Beyond the residential section was her parents' diner, the Tundra, which boasted Scranton's only video game. Joanne smiled as she recalled all the problems they had encountered getting Pac-Man shipped up North.

There was probably a huge bunch of kids waiting to play it at that very moment.

Farther down the road was Scranton's post office. Joanne could imagine its American flag waving gaily in the breeze. Then came the general store, where Scrantonites bought everything from nails to pots and pans and newspapers. Beyond that was the tiny grocery store that sold canned and dried foods, a few terribly overpriced fruits and vegetables, shipped from California, and staples such as bread, cold cuts, and cheese.

The short period when Alaskan vegetables were in season was the time Joanne loved best. The vegetables grew unusually large because in the summer the sun shone most of the day, with only a few hours of darkness. But the season for native produce was short because in the winter it was dark almost all the time and the plants didn't get enough light. Joanne thought about being able to eat fresh fruits and vegetables every day in California. That would be a real treat.

The diner, the post office, the general store, and the grocery store were the only shops in Scranton. There were no bookstores, no boutiques, not even a pizza parlor. People bought their clothes by mail order or picked up socks or a flannel shirt at the general store. Things like cosmetics, medicine, and books all had to be bought in the neighboring town. Since more people lived there, a lot more goods were available. But in the middle of winter the trip was often impossible.

Past the grocery store was the school, which had only four rooms. All Joanne's friends would be there for the first day of school on Monday. She and Maya always started off the school year by making a big breakfast for a few of their closest friends. Then they'd all walk over to school together. She thought of Danny, who lived in the last house before the blacktop headed off into the empty Alaskan landscape. If either of them had been a little bolder, they would have made a great couple. Now they probably wouldn't have the chance. She missed his smile.

"Are you all right, dear?" The woman sitting next to Joanne was looking at her with concern.

"I'm fine," Joanne said firmly, shaking the memories of the town and friends she loved out of her head. This was no time for homesickness. She was excited about going to live in California, and she wasn't going to let any nostalgia for home creep in and ruin that feeling.

To get her mind off her homesickness, she decided to think about the things she didn't like about Scranton. For one thing, it wasn't particularly thrilling. Nothing new ever happened there. Life was very quiet and predictable. But the worst part was, the school didn't have an art teacher. In fact, Joanne was Scranton's only serious artist. She'd taught herself everything she knew by painting and experimenting on her own, reading every art book in the school's tiny library and having long discussions with Mr. Clark, the history teacher who had studied some art history in college.

These thoughts made Joanne remember the long walks she loved to take through the grass and tundra. Bringing her sketchbook with her, she would find a peaceful spot and spend hours drawing the barren landscape. She loved the vast expanse of space, the sky stretching end-lessly above it. In her mind's eye she could see a few birds soaring through the air, chasing the snowy clouds. The coloring was marvelous, the subtle reds and muted oranges of the earth, the bright green of the grass. Here and there would grow a twisted, gnarled tree, stunted by the wind so that it stood only about four feet high.

Alaska was so unlike the pictures of California's lush, gigantic forests or large bustling cities. Joanne knew sketching landscapes wasn't the usual activity California kids chose for fun. They had so many other activities to choose from. But in Scranton the simple things were all they had.

No! Joanne commanded herself. *You're not in Scranton anymore, so don't think about it. Think about California. Think about new adventures.* She turned to her seatmate and smiled. "So tell me about New Falls," she said.

"Dear," the woman said warmly, "I think you're going to love it!"

Wow, it's noisy here, Joanne thought as she stepped off the plane in California. Because of the sounds of the airport and the nearby freeway, she could barely hear the flight attendant wishing her a pleasant stay. She paused on the stairs and took a look around her. Past the flat pavement of the airport were gently rolling hills and tall trees pointing proudly to the sky. *Trees!* Joanne thought. *Real trees, not the poor stunted ones we have in Alaska. How beautiful! And the weather!* She shrugged out of her sweater happily and walked down the steps. *No more ski jackets, no more heavy boots.*

From the pictures her grandparents had sent her, she could imagine what lay unseen in the distance. Scattered among the hills were large, luxurious, modern houses, each one a different shape and style. Somewhere beyond lay New Falls itself, with equally magnificent houses packed closer together. It amazed Joanne to think of how many people must live there, how many streets she'd have to get to know, how many ways there were to get lost in the huge suburbs.

"Joanne, dear," came a woman's call from across the airport pavement.

Joanne spotted her grandparents, and pulling herself out of her California daydream, she ran to them. "Hi," she said breathlessly. "I got a little sidetracked, looking at the view."

Joanne's grandfather laughed. "Understandable. When we first moved down here from Alaska, we spent the whole ride into New Falls with our mouths hanging open. You probably forgot all about your old grandparents when you got a glimpse of those golden hills."

"Oh, of course not," Joanne said with a smile, putting down her carry-on bag and hugging both her grandparents. "It's great to see you. We miss you between your visits to Scranton."

"We miss you, too," Mrs. Trask said. "But we're glad to do without Alaskan winters."

"Welcome to New Falls," Mr. Trask said heartily. "We're so happy to have you down here for a long visit. And we're sure you're going to love California."

Joanne beamed at her grandparents. "I know I will. I've been dreaming about coming here for months."

"Well, let's go," said Mr. Trask, picking up

Joanne's bag. "You're probably exhausted from the trip."

"Actually," Joanne admitted, "I'm more excited than exhausted. I'd love to get a look at my new home."

The Trasks got Joanne's trunk from the airport conveyor belt, another contraption Joanne rarely saw in Alaska, and loaded the luggage into their car. Then they headed down the freeway toward New Falls.

"There's so much traffic." Joanne coughed with surprise at the fumes that rose up from the road. *Something else to get used to*, she thought to herself.

As they drove through the center of New Falls, Joanne's grandmother pointed out the town's landmarks. But Joanne was more interested in things like the huge supermarket, almost a block long, the rows of boutiques filled with fashionable clothes, and the library, which Joanne knew would be packed with books on every imaginable subject. These were the wonderful extras of her trip to New Falls to study art—the things she'd always dreamed of, the things Scranton would never have. Just thinking about them was breathtaking.

They passed through the town and continued down a road dotted with palm trees. Joanne knew that her grandparents' home was about two miles from the center of town but within walking distance of New Falls High.

"There's the mall over there." Mrs. Trask pointed to a modern, two-story building in the middle of a huge, concrete parking lot. "You'll find that's the real center of town. Parents go there to shop, and teenagers go there to meet their friends."

Joanne glanced at her grandmother doubtfully, certain that she was exaggerating. With the gorgeous sunny California weather, why would people spend their time indoors? Joanne looked out once more at the tall, lush trees and the clear sky.

Then Mr. Trask drove by New Falls High, and Joanne peered eagerly out the window at her new school. It was a pretty red-brick building with a large lawn and carefully manicured shrubs. But what struck Joanne the most was its size. "Wow, it's huge!" she cried in amazement.

"Don't worry, dear," Mrs. Trask said kindly. "I'm sure you'll adjust beautifully."

But Joanne knew that over two thousand kids went to school there and she wouldn't know a single one of them. She'd be completely on her own. As her grandfather headed home, Joanne felt her first pang of real panic. Once again she wondered if she'd really be able to fit in with the kids there. Maya had been to the Midwest, and she'd said that people had teased her about being from the boondocks. Would kids at this school do the same to her? Would that prevent her from making new friends? Joanne worried about that for a little while, then did her best to brush aside her fears, losing herself again in the beauty of the scenery and the excitement of a new life and new experiences.

At last Mr. Trask turned the car down a charming little road lined with arching trees and flowering hedges. Pulling up in front of one of the houses, he stopped the car and said, "Well, this is it, Joanne. Your new home for a year."

Joanne jumped out of the car excitedly. Her grandparents' cozy two-bedroom house was made of natural redwood. It was larger and more luxurious than the homes in Scranton, but it wasn't like the fancy, futuristic houses Joanne had seen on the drive over. She was glad about that. The place looked homey, and she knew she'd feel comfortable there.

Joanne and her grandfather unloaded the trunk and brought it into the house. Then the Trasks gave Joanne a tour of their home. The living room had a large stone fireplace and a mixture of old-fashioned and modern furniture. The cheery kitchen was equipped with every convenience and gadget Joanne had ever imagined.

And the walls of the den were lined with all the books Joanne had loved to look at as a child.

And finally Joanne was led to her new room. Her grandparents had decorated it especially for her, with a canopied bed, a large, modern oak desk, a stereo, and two comfortable chairs. "We didn't know what kind of music you like to listen to, so we left the record buying to you," Mr. Trask said lovingly.

"Oh," Joanne said, speechless for a moment at how thoughtful her grandparents had been. "It's beautiful! It's perfect! I love it! I've always wanted a canopied bed. And this is a gorgeous desk. Oh, and the stereo. Grandma, Grandpa, you shouldn't have."

"Now don't go spoiling our fun," Mr. Trask said, smiling. "We enjoyed buying that stereo as much as you'll enjoy using it."

"You two are the greatest grandparents in the whole world," Joanne cried, hugging them both. "Thank you so much for everything—for having me down here, too."

Mr. Trask returned Joanne's hug. "Our pleasure, honey. We're lucky ourselves to be able to have you around for a whole year. And we're glad we can give you the opportunity to see a piece of the world outside of Scranton."

"That's one of the reasons why I'm here," Joanne admitted. "I know I'm sheltered in

Scranton, even though I love it. But of course my main reason is the art classes. I can't wait!"

"Well, school begins soon enough," Mrs. Trask said. "For now, let's show you some of the sights. How about starting with lunch at our favorite fish restaurant?"

"Great. I hear California's fish are just as good as ours." Joanne started to grab her jacket before following her grandparents out of the room.

"You won't need that, dear," Mrs. Trask reminded her.

"I forgot." Joanne laughed. "I guess that's a Scranton habit I'll have to break."

The restaurant was not much larger than a shack, with rough wooden tables set outside under a striped canvas canopy. But the Trasks told Joanne it had the freshest fish in the area. There was also a stunning view of the beach, which was worth the price of the meal itself.

Naturally the California beach was different from the shore in Alaska. The coloring was more brilliant. And, of course, the water in Alaska was usually much too cold for swimming.

The simple, unpretentious restaurant, the gentle slapping of the surf against the sand— Joanne loved it all. She imagined that this would be a place where she'd come often. Let the others spend their days in the mall, she'd spend hers outside, with the sun and waves for company.

"Joanne," Mrs. Trask said, breaking into her granddaughter's thoughts, "perhaps you and I should go shopping tomorrow. You probably need some new clothes."

Just then the food was served, so Joanne and Mrs. Trask never made any plans. That was fine with Joanne. Whenever they had some free time, they'd do it. No hurry. Clothes weren't on the top of her list.

The fish was definitely delicious. The restaurant was a perfect way to cap off a perfect welcome to California. As she stuffed herself, Joanne thought about all the considerate things her grandparents had done for her already in only one afternoon. They were terrific.

Well, I really like California so far, Joanne decided. *We'll see if I feel this good tomorrow, after a full day of school.*

Chapter Two

Joanne's first thought when she got to school the next day was *I'm never going to fit in here.* Suddenly all her excitement of the day before was gone. She gazed at the group of kids standing in front of the school building, all deeply engrossed in conversations about their summer vacations and about which couples had broken up and who had gotten together over the past few weeks. The fashions she saw ran the gamut from neatly pressed pin-striped shirts to hot pink miniskirts and black leather pants. But whatever their style, the kids all seemed very certain of themselves.

Joanne peered down at her own clothes, a shapeless navy sweater over a plain skirt and blouse. Her clothes made her look exactly like what she was—a small-town kid. Appearances weren't very important in Scranton. Mail-order clothes didn't make for high fashion. If the clothes fit, it was rare. If they didn't, you just wore them anyway. But here, her badly fitting clothes made Joanne blush with embarrassment.

She turned her attention to the school building. The brick structure intimidated her almost as much as the sophisticated students standing in happy groups. It was so big, she was sure she'd get lost as soon as she went in. She glanced around hesitantly. All the kids were too busy talking to their friends to notice a shy newcomer. No one even smiled at her, let alone came up and started a conversation. *Oh, well*, Joanne said to herself, *I might as well go in. I'm not getting anything done out here.*

Joanne mounted the school's front steps and pushed the heavy metal doors open. She was supposed to report to the principal's office. But where was it? Long, dull green corridors stretched in three directions.

"Excuse me," Joanne said to a tall boy with a New Falls High jacket around his shoulders. But the boy just hurried past without a glance.

Joanne tried again, this time asking a girl with a short, spiky haircut. She rushed her words to get the whole sentence out before the girl passed her by. "Excuse me, but where's the principal's office?"

The girl stopped, even smiled a little. "Down there, at the end of the hall," she said. Then she hurried off.

Wow, people really come and go quickly around here, Joanne thought as she started off in the direction the girl had pointed. Scranton might be the boondocks, but at least people paid a little attention to one another. A new kid at her old school would have been given the royal treatment.

It was pretty easy to find the principal's office because a line of kids stood outside it. A few of them looked as scared as Joanne felt, and she figured they were new, too. They smiled uncomfortably at one another. Some of the others seemed perfectly at home—probably old-timers with schedule problems, she guessed.

Joanne stood patiently. It was funny that there were more kids waiting to see the principal than were in her whole class at home. When her turn came, a principal's assistant gave her a package containing her schedule, locker number and combination, a map of the building, and a booklet with the school rules. There was also information about the sports teams and special clubs.

"This explains everything you need to know," the assistant said. "If you have any questions, ask your teachers. If you have a serious problem, come back here." She wished Joanne luck and then went on to the next person in line.

Joanne took the package into the hallway and looked at it, a little bewildered. She could see she wasn't going to get any help from the kids, so she'd just have to fend for herself. Well, if she was tough enough to get through sixteen Scranton winters, she was tough enough to get through the first day of school at New Falls High!

She found her locker number in the folder and located the locker on the map of the building. Then she straightened her plain white blouse and started off with determination in the right direction.

As Joanne walked toward her locker, she noticed that all the halls and staircases were painted the same dull green. She couldn't help thinking that using different colors for each wing of the building would have made it much easier to get around, as well as being a lot prettier. Ugly or not, though, the corridors were beginning to fill up with students—some hurrying to classes, others lounging by their lockers, casually talking to friends.

Joanne finally made it to the section of lockers that would include hers. "Let's see," she muttered to herself. "Eight-eighty-one—eight-eighty-two—here, eight-eighty-three." Once again she thumbed through her folder and found the combination. "OK, right thirty-one, left to five, then right again to sixteen," she said out loud, then gave the lock a yank. It didn't budge. "Hmmm." Joanne tried the combination again, but it still didn't open. After the third time, she was beginning to get frustrated. "Darn, how do they get these things open?" she said, pounding her fist against the metal door in annoyance.

"Having trouble?" a voice from behind her inquired.

Joanne whirled around to find a petite, red-haired girl standing there. Her smile was open and friendly. Joanne pointed to the offending locker. "I've been trying to get this thing to work for ten minutes. At this rate I'll never get to class."

"Those old lockers can stick sometimes," the girl said. "Here, let me give you a hand. You must be new."

Does it show that much? Joanne wondered as she handed the girl the piece of paper with the combination on it. She watched her just a little bit enviously. This girl was definitely *not* new. She had a self-assured air about her, as if she knew exactly what she was doing. She was wearing a yellow and black plaid skirt, topped by a baggy black sweater. Her yellow-studded belt was worn low, over her hips, and she had on low-heeled, pointy-toed black boots. Joanne looked down at her own mail-order outfit, feeling embarrassed once again.

"Thirty-one right," the girl said. "Then all the way around left and back to five, then sixteen right. There you go." She slid the lock open easily.

"Oh," Joanne said. "I—I guess I forgot to go all the way around before the second number." She could feel her face blushing bright red. How was she supposed to know things like that?

"Don't worry about it. New schools are always a little confusing. By the way, my name's Rusty."

"I'm Joanne."

"Nice to meet you. So where are you from?"

"Up north," Joanne answered. "Alaska, actually."

"Wow!" Rusty said. "Have you still got all your fingers and toes?"

Joanne laughed. She liked this girl's straightforward, spunky style. "It's really not that cold. I mean, it is, but you get used to it. Hey, thanks for helping me with my locker. If you hadn't come along, I might have been here all day."

"It's OK. I know how it is to be a new kid around here. When my family moved to New Falls two years ago, I really felt out of it. The styles were all different, and so was the music everyone liked. Talking to the other kids was sort of like learning a whole new language."

"Really?" Joanne burst out. "You mean I'm not the only one?"

Rusty grinned. "No way. Changing schools is a bad scene for everyone. Listen, I've got to get to class, but I'll look for you in the cafeteria. What period do you have lunch?"

"Fourth."

"Great, me, too. See you then. Bye, Joanne." And then Rusty was off, rushing down the hall like all the other students.

Joanne found her way down the maze of corridors to her class. Art techniques, with Ms. Statman. *This is it*, she said to herself. *My first real art class*. If it was good, it would make up for everything. With a trembling hand, she pushed open the door.

The classroom was brightly lit, with easels scattered in a rough circle. Paint of every color was spattered on the floor, and the shelves, which ran from floor to ceiling, held art supplies of all descriptions. The first bell had just sounded, so about twenty-five kids were already seated on high stools. Joanne found an empty one and perched nervously on it.

As they waited for the teacher to arrive, Joanne checked out the other students in the class. They were definitely a mixed bunch. One boy sported two-tone hair, while another was busy punching numbers into his pocket calculator. Two girls in alligator shirts talked noisily about a sailing trip they'd been on.

But the person who really caught Joanne's eye was a tall, willowy girl with long blond hair that flowed down her back. Her blue eyes stared out of her tanned, high-cheekboned face as if nothing could faze her. She was wearing tight designer jeans and a New Falls High cheerleader's jacket. Joanne thought she was the most beautiful girl she'd ever seen.

"Hey, Skye," a muscular boy in sweat pants called to her. "You practicing for cheerleader tryouts yet?"

"Hardly," the beautiful girl replied frostily. "I was head cheerleader last year, so I don't have to audition." With a toss of her hair, she turned away.

Joanne watched as Skye got a file out of her bag and began to shape her nails. *Skye—what a gorgeous name*, Joanne thought. *It's perfect for her. She's probably got this whole school wrapped around her little finger. That's probably the way you've got to be around here*, she decided. *Incredibly beautiful, very certain of yourself, and just the tiniest bit nasty.*

At that moment the door opened, and a black-haired boy strolled in. He was tall, with a muscular but slim frame. He was wearing jeans, running shoes, and a blue and white pin-striped shirt. He looked right at Joanne, smiled, then glanced around to find an empty stool. He took one right across the room from her. It gave her a good chance to study him.

He had dark skin, but his cheeks were flushed slightly as if he were happy about something. *Why, he's as excited to be here as I am*, Joanne thought. His black hair just covered the tips of his ears and then curled softly at the nape of his neck. His green eyes were shaded by long, thick eyelashes. He didn't have typical good looks, Joanne decided, but he was definitely cute.

Joanne was so busy staring at the boy that she didn't see the teacher come in. "Hi, I'm Ann Statman. Sorry I'm late," the short, young woman said, throwing some books and packages of art supplies on her desk. "They changed the room, and I got a little lost on my way over. After two years teaching here, these halls still all look the same to me."

Joanne smiled to herself. Boy, did she know what Ms. Statman meant! She had a feeling she was going to like this teacher. For one thing, Ms. Statman didn't look cool and composed like everyone else Joanne had seen so far. A lock of dark blond hair had escaped from her ponytail, and it hung in her eyes. The way she had thrown everything on her desk, she didn't seem very organized.

But once she got the class started, Ms. Statman was anything but disorganized. She immediately drew the students to her. Instead of lecturing to them, telling them what they would and wouldn't be doing, she asked them to introduce themselves and explain why they were taking the class. She really seemed to care about their reasons.

The answers were as varied as the kids in the class. A lot were interested in art but had never worked very seriously at it before. A few, like Skye, said they needed a nonacademic credit and art was as good a choice as any. But Joanne's favorite answer came from the dark-haired boy.

"My name is Tony Corda," he said, "and I'm taking this class because I'd rather be painting or drawing than anything else in the world."

"Great, Tony," Ms. Statman replied. "That's the kind of response that makes me glad to be an art teacher. But we'll be doing a lot more than just painting and drawing. By the end of the year, you'll have learned etching and printing techniques and how to use a variety of materials for sculpture."

When it was Joanne's turn, she glanced nervously at Tony and swallowed the lump in her throat. "I'm Joanne Trask, and I just moved here from Alaska." She heard a snicker from somewhere over her left shoulder and rushed on to cover up the teasing laugh. "Anyway, I guess I feel a lot like Tony about painting and drawing. I really love doing them."

That snicker. It was just what Maya had warned her about. It certainly didn't feel good, especially since she was already nervous about fitting in. But there was nothing she could do about it. Besides, no one else seemed to have heard. Might as well just let it go.

Ms. Statman smiled. "Nice to have you with us, Joanne. I hear it's very beautiful in Alaska."

"It is," Joanne replied shyly. Well, that made her feel a little better. But it was Tony's grin that really cheered her up. As she glanced across the room at him, he gave her a thumbs-up sign.

"How interesting," a bold voice said from the back of the room. Joanne turned to find that the speaker was Skye. The beautiful girl smiled sweetly at her. "You must be very excited to be here."

"I am," Joanne said, happy that the girl seemed interested in her.

"New Falls is a great place to live, too," Skye continued. "I'm sure you'll like it. Maybe I can show you around sometime."

Joanne smiled timidly. She felt shy with this

attractive, obviously popular girl. Joanne couldn't imagine having the guts to speak up in the middle of a class like that. And Skye had done so just to be friendly to her! That more than made up for the snicker.

Her nervousness began to fade quickly—until she heard a boy near her whisper quietly to his friend. "Good old Skye," he said. "She never can stand to have anyone upstage her. She always has to be the center of attention. She was probably just playing up to the teacher with that comment, making sure everyone noticed the class star."

Joanne felt as if she'd had the breath sucked out of her. She wasn't sure whether to believe what the boy said or not. Certainly there was no real reason for Skye to be friendly to her, so maybe it was true. But then, maybe the boy was just nasty or jealous. Maybe he was even the one who had laughed at her.

Joanne didn't know what to think. But she didn't want to believe something so selfish about Skye. She had so much charisma. And she just might be Joanne's second friend, after Rusty, at New Falls High.

Joanne was so wrapped up in her thoughts that she hardly heard the rest of the introductions. She did get more attentive when Ms. Statman began to explain clean-up procedures and how to care for certain materials. Ms. Statman went on to describe the first required project, a series of pen-and-ink drawings using one theme. As the class progressed, Joanne found herself liking the teacher more and more. Here, at last, was someone who could really teach her about art. And she was nice, too. But despite her interest in the lecture, Joanne found herself thinking about Skye all through the period. Had she really meant what she'd said about showing her around?

She also found herself glancing at Tony a lot. There was something that made him different from the other kids. It wasn't just the way he had smiled at her when everyone but Rusty and Skye had looked right past her. It wasn't the way his green eyes sparkled with enthusiasm. It wasn't that he seemed genuinely engrossed in what Ms. Statman was saying, unlike a lot of the other kids. Joanne just couldn't put her finger on what it was.

At last the bell rang. "We have a lot to cover tomorrow," Ms. Statman said. "Don't be late." And then the whole class gathered up their books and rushed off to their next classes.

Joanne picked her bag up slowly, still thinking about Ms. Statman's lecture. When she looked up, Tony was staring right at her. "Bye," he called to her before he strolled into the hallway.

Joanne blushed furiously, and she knew she must be grinning like mad. Suddenly she knew what was different about Tony. *He isn't in a hurry*, she said to herself. *He takes his time. Just like me.*

Chapter Three

After school on Wednesday, Joanne went over to Rusty's house, supposedly to study French. But they weren't getting much work done. Rusty's idea of studying was snacking on fattening foods while listening to loud rock music. Joanne really didn't mind at all. She was just thankful to have Rusty for a friend. She could do her French homework later!

"So, what do you think of New Falls so far?" Rusty asked, reaching for another chocolate cookie.

"I like it," Joanne said, her mouth full. "But I have to admit, sometimes I feel a little lost. It seems as though all people do here is rush from one place to another. I guess I'm just not used to the pace."

"Don't worry, you'll fall right in with the rest of

us soon enough," Rusty assured Joanne. She was sprawled comfortably on her bed while Joanne sat casually on the white shag carpet.

"I've definitely seen a lot of incredible things already," Joanne admitted. "You probably don't realize how different a school like New Falls High is for me. So many facilities, so many kids. Sometimes, when I'm in the cafeteria, I just want to meet everyone in sight."

"You won't feel like that if you ever get stuck in a food fight. That's one experience you ought to try to miss." Rusty leaned forward and slid a tape into the tape deck on her night table. An old Rolling Stones song came pouring out of the speakers.

"I checked out one of the art museums yesterday, and it was really magnificent. And this house! Oh, Rusty, it's just too gorgeous."

Joanne was a little awed by Rusty's house. It was the fanciest home she'd ever been in. It had a Jacuzzi in the bathroom, a living room with sixteen-foot ceilings and a skylight, and a game room with a Ping-Pong table and an extensive video system. Rusty's room looked to Joanne like a cross between a bedroom and a greenhouse. It had huge bay windows with plants sitting on three levels of shelves across the glass.

Joanne was a little awed by Rusty, too. She didn't make a big deal about anything, and she always seemed to have a snappy comeback, no matter what anyone said.

"Thanks. I love this house, too," Rusty said, tossing her orange hair casually. She got up from the bed to adjust the sound of the music. "Can you believe that George Siropa?" Rusty asked Joanne over her shoulder. "That's the boy who came up to us as we were leaving school and tried to get us to have a conversation with him. He'll do anything to get voted into the student council, even talk to me. We pretty much hate each other," she explained to Joanne.

"You certainly told him where to go," Joanne said. She took another cookie, dipped it into her milk, and took a bite.

Rusty had looked George coolly in the face and said, "I'm voting for Mary Govern for student council, so just forget it." Poor George. With those words, he had deflated like a leaky balloon. It certainly hadn't been nice of Rusty, but Joanne could appreciate what her friend had done. Joanne herself probably would have politely let a guy like George talk for hours, no matter what other things she'd had planned.

Joanne saw that Rusty really knew how to take care of herself. People didn't mess around with her or try to take advantage of her. They probably didn't dare to.

And Joanne knew she could learn a few things

from her new friend's attitude. She had heard a couple of nasty comments in the past three days, remarks about the new Eskimo girl and stuff like that. It wasn't that Joanne would be embarrassed to be thought an Eskimo. The northern Indians had a beautiful culture, one they had every reason to be proud of. But the comments were said in ugly tones, and that bothered Joanne. Especially now, when she didn't have too many friends. In fact, Rusty was it as far as friends went. Skye had never mentioned anything further about showing her around.

So those comments really upset Joanne. The worst of it was, she hadn't known how to react. She had just blushed angrily and said nothing. Joanne could imagine how Rusty would have reacted in the same situation. She would have given the hecklers a piece of her mind, but fast.

Still, there was a tough edge to her new friend, which Joanne didn't quite understand. In a way Rusty tried *too* hard to look as though nothing could possibly upset or worry her. Joanne could see that other kids might be a little turned off by it. It was intimidating. Because if you had doubts or were unsure of yourself, you ended up looking like a wimp in front of Rusty.

Nonetheless, Joanne had to admit that Rusty had been nothing if not kind and encouraging to her. She made sure they ate lunch together, helped her learn her way around school, and included her in her group of friends. The group accepted her because Rusty did.

Rusty sat on the edge of her bed and began to snap her fingers to the beat as a favorite song came on. "So you went to the art museum, huh? You know, I haven't gone in ages. I keep meaning to. My mom's always telling me how beautiful it is."

"Oh, you've got to go, Rusty. It's one of the really special things about New Falls."

"Well, when I have a few spare hours, I'll go check it out."

"Gosh," Joanne said. "I think I could sit in front of some of those paintings for days and not get tired of looking at them."

"You're really into art, aren't you?" Rusty said curiously. "You were absolutely raving about your art class when I saw you at lunch the first day of school. Do you still like it?"

"It gets better and better," Joanne answered. "Ms. Statman always has something interesting to say, and the kids in class are fun to watch, too."

Rusty laughed. "Is it possible, Joanne, that some lucky boy has caught your eye?"

Joanne hesitated, a little embarrassed. How could she tell Rusty about Tony? They hadn't even had a real conversation yet. "Um," she said, stalling. "Actually, I was, uh, thinking about this girl. Her name's Skye. Do you know her?"

"Skye Morrison? Sure, everyone knows her. Or at least they know *of* her. Who could miss her?"

"You don't sound as if you like her too much."

"I don't," Rusty replied in her typical straightforward way. "She's sweet when it suits her purpose, nasty when it's easier to be that way."

"Oh," said Joanne, a little dejected. "The first day of class she said maybe she'd show me around. But she hasn't even said hi to me since. I heard some boy saying she was just being friendly to me to get in good with the teacher. I really hoped she was being sincere."

"Knowing Skye, I doubt it," Rusty said. "It sounds to me as if that boy may be right." Rusty finished her glass of milk and set it down on the night table. "One thing about Skye is that she definitely knows how to get what she wants. She may not be very nice sometimes, but she's got style. Frankly, I admire that. I think knowing how to get what you want is pretty important," Rusty confided. "I try not to let anyone push me around."

"I noticed," Joanne said with a smile.

"You know, I think you could stick up for yourself a little more, Joanne. Some people have to be put in their places."

"What are you talking about?"

"Hey, I heard that kid call you the Eskimo girl at lunch today. I wouldn't have let him get away with that. And neither would Skye. Can you imagine someone insulting Skye that way?"

Joanne thought for a moment. Rusty was right. The idea of it was so absurd, it was almost funny. "I don't know," Joanne said. "It's just not my style, you know? I'm not used to being so tough with people."

"Sure, but it's something you can learn to do."

Joanne shook her head thoughtfully. "I'm just not sure."

"Well, if you decide you want to work on it," Rusty continued, "let me know. I was new here once, too." Her tone softened. "I know what you're going through." The tape finished, and Rusty leaned over to turn off the set. "How about we play a short game of Ping-Pong before we start our French?"

"Sounds good," Joanne said, standing up and stretching.

"I'm very good at putting off conjugating verbs," Rusty said as she pulled herself up from the bed.

"That," Joanne said, "is one talent I'd love to learn from you."

"Only one of many," Rusty said. "Only one of many."

Joanne lost the Ping-Pong game. She hadn't been concentrating very hard. Her mind was filled with Rusty's words. Would acting tough like Rusty help her in her new home? It wasn't like her. Could she learn how? And did she want to?

Chapter Four

It was a few weeks later on a Friday evening that Joanne got her first real taste of Southern California social life. She was sitting high up in the bleachers, ready to take in her first New Falls football game. The game itself hadn't begun yet, but Joanne could feel the excitement in the air. Crowds of noisy kids packed the stands surrounding the field. They were grouped together in twos, threes, tens, all laughing and joking. Their high spirits were contagious, and Joanne felt like laughing with them.

From the snatches of conversations she'd overheard in the cafeteria all week, it seemed as if everyone would be at the game. Unfortunately, Rusty and her friends hadn't been too hot on the idea of coming. They thought the whole sports program was set up for the serious jocks, with nothing at all for people who just wanted to play for fun. "Besides," Rusty's friends had said, "who wants to go watch a bunch of guys sweating all over each other?" "If you've seen one football game, you've seen them all" was their attitude. So they had all stayed home.

But what if you've never seen one of these games? Joanne had said to herself. There sure wasn't a football team in Scranton. There were no facilities for it, no money for a sports program and, most importantly, not enough kids of the right age. The jock types in Scranton didn't have the luxury of playing on a team. They had to content themselves with solo sports like running or cross-country skiing. So Joanne had decided to come to the football game alone, just to see what one was really like.

Of course Joanne had seen some football on TV, but she'd never been interested enough to sit down and watch a complete game. She knew the game would be different live. Being part of the excited, screaming crowds would be great—a lot better than sitting around the living room with the TV on. Maybe now she'd understand why her father had such a thing for Monday night football.

Joanne pushed the thought of her father out of her mind. It would be very easy to get lost in a long, homesick daydream. She missed her parents. She missed Scranton and her friends. It had been a hard few weeks, maybe the hardest of her life. She'd never felt so alone.

It was Rusty who'd really gotten her through it. Rusty, who'd found her every day at lunch, introduced her to her friends, included her in their conversations. She'd never once made fun of all the things Joanne didn't know about and had never seen before. Too bad Rusty wasn't here now!

Joanne shook her head, then brought her attention back to the noisy scene around her. The school band was warming up the crowd with a few lively tunes, but no one was really listening to them. And on the left side of the field, the cheerleading squad was practicing one of their routines. Joanne could see Skye, looking gorgeous as usual, in her short blue and white skirt and cheerleader jacket. Joanne thought the girl had probably never been awkward or unsure of herself in her life.

At that moment the band picked up its pace and began playing the school song. One by one the players ran onto the field while a voice on the P.A. system announced each boy's name, class, and position. Everyone shouted wildly, and the cheerleaders went through a series of perfectly coordinated high kicks and jumps. To Joanne the whole scene looked a little strange.

So, Joanne Trask, she said to herself, *you are about to see your first football game. How does it feel?* She stared gloomily at three girls sitting near her who were cheering madly and laughing together. Joanne answered her own question. *Lonely! Well, no one said spending the year in California would be easy*, she told herself. *I'll find my way. Eventually.*

Joanne knew the experiences she'd have in New Falls would be worth all the difficulties of fitting in. But that thought didn't make her miss her friends from home any less. If only Maya were here. And Danny. With those two, she would have been laughing and yelling just like the rest of the crowd. Right now, though, as she sat by herself and watched the opening plays of the game, she felt terribly lost and alone.

As the game progressed, Joanne began to wish she *had* watched a few games with her father. She couldn't figure out any of the rules, so half the time she had no idea what was going on. There was a lot of standing around and measuring. And when the players did break into a few minutes of action, she couldn't see any pattern or reason to what they were doing.

New Falls seemed to be winning. At least, that's what the scoreboard said. But as the New Falls kids got more and more happy and excited, Joanne felt more and more lonely and depressed. After a while she didn't even watch the game much. She turned her attention to the cheering crowds of spectators. What made them so different from her? It wasn't just that they were with friends and she wasn't.

One thing was certain—she couldn't go around in mail-order clothes any longer. The next day she'd ask her grandmother to take her shopping for some new outfits. Joanne looked around at what the other girls were wearing. She liked the low-heeled boots a lot of them had. Maybe she'd get a pair of those, and she could definitely use some jeans that fit her better than the ones she had on. If she got a skirt, a few smart-looking shirts, and some accessories, she'd have a whole new wardrobe. That wasn't a lot of stuff, so it couldn't cost too much. And it would get her started on a more up-to-date image.

Joanne got so caught up in her thoughts that it was halftime before she knew it. The cheerleaders ran onto the field, Skye leading them. They went into a routine of kicks, splits, and cartwheels, their pom-poms flying. It was a pretty impressive display.

But Joanne's heart sank as she watched Skye kicking her perfectly formed legs high into the air. New clothes or no new clothes, Joanne knew she'd never, ever be anything like this girl with the silky blond hair and the winning smile. The more she watched, the more hopeless she felt. Fitting in at New Falls High was a losing battle. Suddenly she wanted to go home right away. Being in a crowd of happy, cheering people only made her more lonesome.

Joanne slowly picked her way down the bleachers to go home. Her grandparents had been nice enough to lend her the car, but she would have been better off staying home. Who needed football games, anyway? Deep down, Joanne heard herself answer, *You do. You really want to belong in this place.* Dejected, she kicked an empty paper cup out of her way.

"Hey, is that you, Joanne?" came a voice on the bench below her.

Joanne glanced down to see who had called her. It was Tony. "H-hi," she stuttered, her heart pounding excitedly.

"I'm surprised to see you here," he said. "In art class you never seemed like the football type." He motioned for her to sit down next to him.

"I'm not," Joanne admitted, taking a seat. "You may not believe this, but I'd never seen a live football game until today."

Tony laughed. "Too much snow in Alaska for a good scrimmage." He said it with a friendly smile, not in the way some kids teased her, so she didn't mind the joke at all. "So how do you like it?" he asked.

Joanne sighed. "Actually, I'm confused. I mean, are there really any rules to this game, or do they just light the scoreboard whenever they want to hear the crowd scream?"

"Ah," Tony said, running his hand through his black hair, "you're a football novice. Sure there are rules, but they're hard to follow unless someone tells you what they are. It can be pretty frustrating to watch a game without knowing them. I'm amazed you stayed this long."

"Well," Joanne told him, smiling, "I was just on my way home."

"But you're not leaving now!" Tony said emphatically.

"I'm not?"

"Nope. Tony Corda is going to give you your first football lesson. Come on. Let's get close up where you can really see the action."

Tony grabbed Joanne's hand and pulled her to her feet, then led her through the crowd until they were pressed against the fence surrounding the field. Joanne, for her part, was perfectly happy to let Tony lead her along. In fact, she was more than happy. She was ecstatic.

Aside from being extremely cute, he seemed nice, too. He always smiled at her from across the room whenever their eyes met, and they'd talked a little after class. But this was no hallway chitchat. It was more like—an informal date.

Once again the players ran onto the field, and this time Joanne cheered as loudly as everyone else.

Tony pulled her close to him so she could hear what he was saying over the noise of the crowd. "The most important thing about football, Joanne, is not the rules."

"Then what is it?" Joanne asked, enjoying the sensation of Tony's nearness.

"It's the way the players interact with one another. On a good play, they move as smoothly as dancers. You know, some people think football is boring. They say the whole point is to get a piece of stuffed skin over a painted line. It's much more than that."

"So how did you get to be such a big appreciator of the sport?" Joanne asked curiously.

"See the quarterback over there, number thirty-one?"

"Sure," Joanne said, squinting into the sun.

"That's my older brother, Joe."

"You're kidding."

"Nope. He's the athletic one of the family. I'm the artistic one. Now, before they start playing, let me explain the basic rules to you."

The next hour was sheer bliss for Joanne. She wasn't a single in a crowd of twos and threes anymore. She was part of a pair. She had a friend, too, someone with whom to share the highs and lows of the game. And he was a very cute friend at that. *Maybe things are going to work out for me in New Falls,* she thought.

With Tony's help, Joanne began to make sense of the game. Actually the rules were pretty simple. And Tony described the plays as if they were dances. They were, in fact, all planned out, just like ballets. It was the other team's job to search for the flaw in the planning and prevent a goal from being scored.

As it turned out, New Falls lost the game. "What happened?" Joanne asked, confusion in her voice as she stood in front of the bleachers, ready to leave. "They were so far ahead at halftime."

"They got overconfident and stopped concentrating."

"Well, it's too bad, but I enjoyed the game anyway. When you look at it the way you do, it doesn't really matter who wins or loses."

Tony chuckled. "Oh, it matters. My brother is going to be in a terrible mood tonight. If only he could see things *our* way."

Tony smiled, his green eyes meeting Joanne's blue ones. Then slowly, he reached out and took her hand. He didn't do it casually. Joanne was sure it was a very deliberate gesture of friendship. More than friendship.

"Well, well, well," a voice cut in. "It's our little Alaskan artist with Joe's little brother." Skye swept past them, throwing her remarks over her shoulder. "Tony, honey, you'd better watch out, or you might get frostbite."

Joanne quickly snatched her hand from Tony's and turned away so he wouldn't see the hurt in her eyes. The afternoon had been so perfect until Skye had come along.

Clearly embarrassed, Tony kicked a stone at his feet. "Don't mind her," he mumbled uncomfortably. "She's like that sometimes, but she doesn't really mean it. Believe me, she's just upset about losing the game. Sometimes Skye takes out her bad moods on the people around her."

Joanne kept her head bent. "I've been getting teased all the time about where I come from," she confessed. "So I'm supersensitive about it."

"It's not you," Tony insisted. "Skye's having a really hard time lately, and she's been acting pretty nasty. It's nothing personal. She's probably taking things out on you because you're with me and it was my big brother who blew the last play. The whole thing gets kind of involved in a weird way." Then, as if answering Joanne's

49

unasked question, he added, "She dates my brother. That's how I know so much about her."

Joanne raised her head, forcing herself to look into Tony's sensitive green eyes. He was so nice. But his explanation didn't take the sting out of Skye's comment. It hurt especially that it was Skye who'd said it. Skye, who fascinated Joanne so much, who she'd hoped would be her friend. Well, obviously, that boy had been right on the first day of school. Skye hadn't really been interested in her. She'd used her to get attention, to seem considerate and thoughtful to the teacher and the other kids in the class. Joanne should have realized it when Skye hadn't followed through on her invitation to show her around.

Hick! Joanne hated the word, but that was exactly what she felt like when people teased her about Scranton. It was obvious to Skye and all the other kids that Joanne was different, not as sophisticated as they were. And to some of them, that gave them the license to be nasty to her. Joanne didn't like to think about that. She needed some way to deal with the problem, or she'd get pushed around all year. Well, she'd talk to Rusty about it. Maybe her friend would have some advice.

Then Joanne had a terrible thought. Maybe Tony thought of her as a hick, too. Maybe he was just being kind by spending time at the football game with her. She was really beginning to like him. But with all the beautiful, fashionable girls around, why should he go for a small-town kid like her? *The answer*, Joanne told herself, *is he shouldn't.*

"Are you all right, Joanne?" Tony asked with concern.

"Sure," Joanne replied, managing a weak grin. "I guess losing a game is pretty depressing around here."

"It is." He hesitated, then said, "And by the way, Skye knows I hate to be called Joe's little brother, so it wasn't just you she was picking on." He smiled. "Come on, I'll walk you to your car."

Joanne wished the parking lot was five miles away. She didn't want this special time with Tony to end. But all too soon they reached Joanne's car, and the two of them had to say their goodbyes.

As she drove toward her grandparents' house, Joanne didn't quite know what to make of the whole evening. It had flipped from terrible to wonderful and back too many times. She couldn't help cringing at the memory of Skye's snotty comment. And Joanne was sure Tony couldn't like her the way she liked him.

Yet he had seemed very concerned about her. He certainly wouldn't have spent half the game with her if he didn't like her at least a little. And the way he'd taken her hand was not just a friendly gesture. *Maybe there's hope for a special relationship between Tony and me*, she thought.

But Skye's remark had soured the evening for Joanne. In her heart she still felt very much like an outsider.

Chapter Five

Mrs. Trask smoothly pulled the car into one of the empty parking spaces. "Welcome to New Falls mall, the biggest shopping plaza south of L.A.," she said to Joanne breezily. Joanne took a closer look at the building she had passed on her first day in California. It was a large, modern brick structure with arched entrances and attractive windows. "There are indoor streets," Joanne's grandmother added. "With a glass roof on the top floor so you really feel like you're outside."

"That's funny," Joanne said, laughing.

"Why do you think so?" her grandmother asked.

"Wouldn't it have been easier to make real streets? Then, when you wanted to go outside, you'd just go outside."

"Oh," her grandmother exclaimed, "but what about when it rains?"

"You'd get wet, I guess. But it hardly ever rains around here anyway."

"Well, you won't get wet in this mall. Besides, it's a pleasure to shop here. The mall is so clean and carefully maintained. I wish our streets were so well kept."

Joanne shook her head in confusion. What a strange idea. If there was enough money in the town budget for a fancy mall, there was probably enough for a really good street-cleaning drive. And if they'd planted grass instead of paving the area for a parking lot, it would have made a great playing field for kids. But what bothered her the most was that the two-story building blocked out the beautiful view of the golden hills.

"I guess," Joanne mused out loud, "coming from Alaska gives me a different perspective on these things. When there's nothing at all modern where you live, you really learn to appreciate nature. This mall could be anywhere in the world. It doesn't make use of the natural beauty in this area."

"Maybe so," her grandmother said. "But wait and see the stores!"

Inside, the mall was a posh, fashionable shopping district. There were ice-cream stores serving exotic flavors like banana-mango, boutiques selling handmade sweaters, specialty food stores, toy stores, pet stores, furniture shops, pizza parlors—and that was only the beginning. All the stores were designed and decorated with the best of taste, and they sold only top-quality merchandise.

Joanne gasped. "Wow, I had no idea it would be like this. It's kind of like a playground for adults."

Joanne's grandmother laughed. "You could put it that way. You see, I knew you'd like it once you saw the inside."

"There are so many stores, Grandma. Where do we start?" Joanne asked, staring all around her in amazement. For a girl who had lived her whole life in a town with only four stores, the mall was quite a sight.

"One of a Kind Clothing is on the second floor," Mrs. Trask said. "They've got some lovely dresses."

"Great," Joanne said. "Rusty had on a fantastic black turtleneck dress the other day. I'd love something like that."

Joanne and her grandmother rode the escalator to the second floor. That, too, was new for her. "This is great," she said. "The lazy person's way to the top. In Alaska if you want to go up the stairs, you have to use your feet."

Joanne's eyes grew big as they passed shop

after shop filled with pretty clothes. "No more mail order for me," she declared.

The saleswoman in One of a Kind Clothing was about the same age as Joanne's grandmother. "Looking for some new school dresses?" she asked Joanne politely.

"Exactly," Joanne said with a grin. "As you can see, I'm a little out of date."

The woman smiled. "I'm sure we have a few things you'll like. Have a look at this rack."

"Joanne," Mrs. Trask exclaimed, "isn't this outfit just darling?" She held up a simple, light blue dress with a rounded collar and a matching jacket.

Joanne looked at the outfit for a moment. It wasn't at all what she'd had in mind. It was just the kind of thing found in a mail-order catalog. "Well—" she hesitated.

"Oh, come on, dear, try it on. I'm sure it'll be just perfect for you."

"It's not quite—" Joanne began nervously, twisting the end of her braid. She didn't want to try the awful dress on, but she didn't want to hurt her grandmother's feelings, either.

"You'll never know what it looks like until you slip into it," the saleswoman said. "I think your grandmother has very good taste. This is just the kind of outfit I wore as a young girl."

Joanne groaned to herself. If it wasn't so

ironic, it would be funny. Here she was, shopping for new fashioned clothes, and she was stuck with two very old-fashioned women giving her advice. She should have figured her grandmother wouldn't be the right person to go shopping with.

"You know, Grandma," Joanne said diplomatically, "I just realized that I need a lot of things more than I need a pretty dress like that. For instance, I could really use some nice shoes to replace these old sneakers and some jeans that fit me better than these. Maybe we should come back here after we've gotten some of the other things I really need."

"That sounds very sensible," Mrs. Trask said. "We'll be back," she said and smiled at the saleswoman. Joanne let out a sigh of relief and congratulated herself on getting out of a sticky situation.

But now that she knew she couldn't trust her grandmother's judgment on where to shop, Joanne was at a loss. Where should they go next? "Grandma," she suggested, "why don't we just walk around a bit and take a look at what stores are here? I'm pretty amazed at how many different places there are."

As they strolled along the indoor streets, a surprise awaited Joanne around every corner. The funniest shop, she decided, was a store called

Recline. It sold nothing but vinyl beach chairs. Another favorite was the Balloon Store, where customers could order bouquets of brightly colored balloons instead of flowers.

And then, at the very end of one street, Joanne saw the perfect shoe store. Its windows were lined with shoes of every color. They had seven different shades of the leather pumps so many of the girls at school wore, and five shades of the rubber-tipped sneakers that were another popular style. And right in front of the window sat a row of the low-heeled boots Joanne knew she wanted.

"Let's take a look in here," she said casually to her grandmother.

The boots fit perfectly when Joanne tried them on. They were almost as comfortable as sneakers, and they looked a lot better. Joanne figured she could wear them both with pants and with dresses. And the price was right.

Now came the hard decision—what color? Joanne almost chose the purple ones but then decided they were too flashy for her. She definitely wasn't sure enough of her new style to call attention to herself. In the end she took a charcoal gray pair and wore them out of the store.

"They're lovely," Mrs. Trask said once they were out in the glass-roofed street. "The leather is so soft, and the color is just right. They'll go with everything."

Joanne scolded herself for putting down her grandmother's taste without really giving her a chance. "Thanks," she said. "Do you know, this is the first item for my wardrobe I've ever picked out all by myself? Mom always did most of the choosing. It didn't really matter, anyway. We weren't much for dressing up back in Alaska."

"Then I'm proud of you, Joanne. You've got a good eye for style." It was the nicest thing her grandmother could have said to her.

They wandered down a few more streets until Joanne got sidetracked in an art supply store. It was absolutely huge, and it smelled of paint. Just looking at all the different materials gave her new ideas for her project in art class. They had already started working with pen and ink, but Joanne had never imagined that there were so many different shapes and sizes of pens. And the rainbow of ink colors stretched all the way across the display counter. She bought two pens and some vermilion ink and then set about browsing happily through the store.

"Hey, Joanne," came a friendly call. Joanne turned to find Rusty peeking through the door of the art supply store, her hair braided in six or seven tiny plaits. "I recognized your braid from the back," she said. "See, we match today." She held out one of her own braids. "So what are you up to?"

"I'm doing a little shopping with my grandmother and finding out about the wonders of a Southern California mall. It's really neat here."

"That's right," Rusty said. "I forgot that you've probably never seen anything like this. When you've grown up with it all your life, it's nothing special. Just another boring Saturday at the mall." She glanced down at Joanne's feet. "Hey, new boots."

"I bought them about ten minutes ago," Joanne said, lifting her pant legs to give her friend a better look.

"I like 'em, I like 'em. Listen, do you still have some more shopping to do, or can you come get an ice cream with me?"

Joanne turned to her grandmother, who had strolled over to where the girls stood. "Go ahead, Joanne. I've got a few errands to do. Meet me here in an hour, and we'll buy you a few more things." She gave Joanne a kiss on the forehead and waved the girls out of the store. "In an hour," she called after them.

A few minutes later Joanne and Rusty were seated comfortably at the ice-cream parlor, waiting for the waitress to bring them the desserts they had ordered. "So what other clothes are you going to buy today?" Rusty asked.

"Some jeans and shirts. I'll come back for dresses and skirts another day."

"We should come together. I love shopping with a friend."

"Great, I could use your advice on what to get."

"I'll give you some right now. When you're buying jeans, get black ones. They're just as comfortable as the regular kind, but they look about fifty times better. Any shirt looks great with them. I'm telling you, my black jeans are my best friends."

The waitress hurried over, two dishes balanced skillfully in one hand. "Apple cinnamon for you," she said, placing a dish in front of Joanne. "And orange chocolate for you." She set the other one by Rusty. "Enjoy."

"Thanks," the girls replied.

"This place is absolutely the best!" exclaimed Rusty. "They make the ice cream right in the back of the store. It's not factory made or anything."

Joanne laughed. "Actually, that's not such a big deal to me. Homemade ice cream is the only kind we get up in Scranton. It's too expensive to fly it in, so if we want it, we have to make it ourselves. But," she added, taking a bite of her apple cinnamon, "this is delicious!"

"Hey, I never thought of that," said Rusty, digging into her ice cream, too. "You know, it's weird, Joanne. The things I think are so ordinary, like the mall or a football game, are totally new and really impressive to you. But then there are other things you've had all your life that we suburban kids missed out on, like homemade ice cream and small classes at school."

"I've been thinking about that, too. You've got a lot of conveniences and entertainment here, but you miss out on some of the simpler pleasures. I mean, if we were in Scranton, we wouldn't be in a plush mall where we could buy things from all over the world. We'd probably be hiking to Nickerson's Pond. Both are fun. I don't think one is more fun—just different."

"Do you miss home a lot?" Rusty asked.

"Yes and no," Joanne replied, swirling her ice cream around in the dish. "I'm glad I'm here, but sometimes I get awfully homesick. Just seeing Maya and Danny and my parents for ten minutes would make me incredibly happy. Letters can help, but it's still hard. Especially when I start feeling like I'll never fit in at New Falls High."

"You will," Rusty assured her. "All you need is time."

Joanne sighed. "Sometimes I think it's impossible to make any friends here."

"You've got me," Rusty said, spooning ice

:ream into her mouth. "And my friends like you, oo."

"Yes, but—" Joanne broke off quickly.

"But there's someone special you want to get o know," Rusty said, a twinkle in her eye. Maybe a guy?"

"Kind of," Joanne replied, blushing scarlet. She decided to confide in Rusty about Tony. "It's a boy in my art class. He always stops to talk to ne, and we have some good conversations, and I hink he might even be interested in me," she aid in a rush of words. "But I'm just not sure if 'm his type," she finished abruptly.

"Whoa, slow down." Rusty laughed. "First of ll, what's his name?"

"Tony Corda."

"Oh, I know him a little. He seems nice."

"I think so, too." Joanne sighed, her ice cream orgotten. She recounted the whole story of the ootball game, including Skye's nasty comment nd Tony's reaction to it.

"Hey, don't look so crushed," Rusty said when Joanne had finished. "It sounds like pretty good news to me." She smiled encouragingly at Joanne. "Now you'd better eat that ice cream before it melts."

Joanne appeased her friend by taking two big bites. It really was good. "How so?" she asked.

"Well, no guy holds a girl's hand if he doesn't

like her. And it sounds as though he was really worried about Skye hurting your feelings."

"You really think so?" Joanne burst out happily.

"Sure," Rusty answered. "But hold on a minute. There's more to it than that. Having a guy like you is only the first step. You've got to keep his interest and make it grow. I can think of a million relationships that fizzled out before they even got started."

"A million?" Joanne asked skeptically.

"Well, half a million." Rusty laughed. "But anyway, I think you have a point about Tony maybe liking more sophisticated girls. After all, his brother dates Skye, so he's used to having a girl like her around. She's a role model to him for what a girlfriend should be."

"You mean, you think he'll want a girlfriend just like his big brother's?"

"Exactly," Rusty said, nodding her head vigorously.

"Then I'm sunk. I'll never be as sophisticated as Skye."

"Sure you can be. All you need is a new wardrobe, a crash course in popular culture, and a whole lot of practice."

"Rusty, please," Joanne said, laughing. "By the time I've done all that, we'll be in our midthirties."

"No way. It's easy. The secret is, you need to be just a little bit tough." Rusty leaned forward to emphasize what she was about to say. "If you're gentle, the way you are, people like Skye are going to step all over you."

"But you didn't."

"Yeah, well, I'm an exception. When Skye treats you badly, you have to give it right back to her. You'll get her off your back, and at the same time you'll impress Tony with the way you handle difficult situations."

"Like how?" Joanne asked. She wasn't quite sure what her friend meant.

"Well, after that frostbite remark, you could have said something like, 'I'm not the only ice queen around here.' "

"Oh, Rusty, that's a terrible pun, and it's mean, too."

"But at least you would have shown Tony that you can't be pushed around."

"But I can be."

"Only if you let yourself be," Rusty stated firmly.

"But, don't you see, it's hopeless." Joanne groaned. "I'd never even seen a mall before today. There must be a million things you take for granted that I don't even know exist."

"Probably not that many. You've seen video arcades, right?"

"We have a machine at the diner in Scranton, but I've never been to one of those places that has dozens of games."

"I'll take you to one. What about MTV?"

"Well, I've heard about it, even seen some of the videos, but we only get three TV stations in Scranton, so we don't get MTV as a regular program."

"I can't believe it. You'll have to come to my place and watch it. You've been to rock concerts, haven't you?"

"Um, I'm afraid not too many bands get out to Scranton."

"That's easy enough to fix. The Ex-Zombies are playing next month at the Palace Theatre. You'll come with me and the rest of the gang. You've heard of the Ex-Zombies, haven't you?"

"I've got to admit that I haven't. If they're not on top twenty radio or have a really popular record out, we probably don't know them in Scranton."

"I'm shocked. Joanne, you have a lot to learn, but luckily, you've found the right girl to teach you. Me! So don't despair. Tony Corda is not going to know what hit him when I get done with you. You'll out-Skye Skye, but you'll be nicer than she is."

"I don't know, Rusty. There's a reason why

Skye treats me like a know-nothing small-town girl."

"There is?"

"Yes. I *am* one."

"Not for long. Joanne Trask, this is where your education really begins."

Chapter Six

Joanne spent Sunday morning relaxing around the house, doing some reading and finishing up a few homework assignments. It was comforting not to be rushing around the way she had been all week. It was just what she would have done on a Sunday in Scranton—except that in California she could lie out in the sun in the backyard in a bathing suit instead of bundling up in a down jacket. She had set up a beach chair, found a pad and pencil, and just settled down to write a letter to Maya when her grandmother came outside and joined her, a cup of coffee in her hand.

"Hi," Joanne said, squinting at her in the sun.

"Hi," Mrs. Trask said, pulling up another beach chair. "What's new?"

"Just about everything," Joanne said and laughed.

"How are things going? You've seemed a little upset this weekend."

"Well," Joanne said, trying to decide whether or not she should tell her grandmother about Skye and Rusty and Tony. She figured she might as well; she needed a little good advice. "Something kind of weird happened to me on Friday."

"Oh?" asked Mrs. Trask with interest.

"Yeah. It's about this guy."

"I should have guessed," Mrs. Trask said almost to herself. "Tell me about him."

"Well, his name is Tony Corda, and he's in my art class. I bumped into him at the football game on Friday, and we had a really good time. I like him a lot, but I'm not sure how he feels about me."

"Go on," Mrs. Trask urged.

"Well, there's also this girl Skye. She's really beautiful but kind of snobby. She said something really nasty to me at the game when I was with Tony."

"And that hurt," Mrs. Trask said.

"Yeah, a lot." Joanne nervously drummed the eraser of her pencil on the pad in front of her. "My friend Rusty says I have to change my attitude, be tougher, take care of myself, and not worry so much about being polite."

"Do you want to do that?" Mrs. Trask asked gently.

"I don't know," Joanne answered. "But Skye's that way, and so is Rusty. They'd never get teased the way I do."

"It seems to me," Mrs. Trask said, "that it won't really work to put on an act that isn't really you. It doesn't make much sense to try and change your whole personality just because a few immature kids make some nasty comments."

"Oh, but it wouldn't be changing my personality, more like changing my style." Joanne was a little annoyed that her grandmother didn't understand that distinction immediately. "I mean, I'm in California now. I can't go around dressing and acting as if I'm still in Scranton."

"Well, are you sure you want to be like Skye?" Mrs. Trask continued. "She may be pretty, but she sounds awfully selfish. If Tony likes girls like that, I'd say he's welcome to them."

"But, Grandma, don't you see?" Joanne cried, frustration creeping into her voice. "I do want to be popular and fashionable and self-confident. I mean, who wouldn't want that? I hate feeling as if everything I do shows that I'm new here and that I'm an outsider. That's why I think Rusty knows what she's talking about. She hasn't been here all that long herself, and she's plenty popular."

"I can understand that, Joanne," Mrs. Trask said. "But I think it's possible to be all those things without being untrue to yourself. I hope you realize that. Anyway, you make your own decision. Just remember, I'm here if you want to talk or if you need some advice." Mrs. Trask drained the last of her coffee. She got up quickly, kissed the top of Joanne's head, and walked into the house.

Joanne sighed. She wasn't at all sure who was right. And she was having an awful time trying to figure things out for herself. She wished someone would just come in, like a fairy god-mother, and drop the best answer in her lap.

She picked up her pencil and began writing to Maya. Maybe getting her thoughts down on paper would help. All she knew right now was that she was very confused.

Monday morning Joanne got dressed in some of the clothes she had bought at the mall. She topped her black jeans with a red-and-white-striped shirt and added her new boots. After combing and braiding her hair, she checked her image in the mirror. Well, she was certainly no Skye, but it felt awfully good to see herself in clothes that didn't come from a two-year-old catalog. This outfit actually did something for her. It sure showed off her figure better than a pair of sloppy jeans or a shapeless skirt. She felt different already—poised and attractive.

When she walked into art class later that morning, she was on top of the world. The new clothes really did make her feel better about herself. A smile on her face, she pushed open the door to the classroom, enjoying the sound of her heels clicking against the linoleum floor. The first person she saw was Tony. He flashed her a big smile.

Ms. Statman rushed into the class just behind Joanne, her arms full of packages as usual. "OK, this is it!" she exclaimed excitedly. "You've practiced enough with pen and ink. You're ready to go on to a real project. Now, what I want is a series of three ink drawings on the same subject. We'll be working on this project for most of the first semester. Today I want you to think about your subject and do a few pencil sketches."

The teacher's enthusiasm was contagious, and Joanne threw herself into her work. First, she did a quick sketch of an Alaskan scene. It was the kind of thing she had loved doing back home. But now the drawing just didn't feel satisfying. It was pretty, but it was the same old scene she'd drawn a hundred times before.

She thought it over. The Alaskan scene had

been perfect when she'd lived in Scranton. But she needed to draw something more connected with her new life in California. She considered doing some sketches of the mall, but she figured three of them would get pretty repetitive.

Suddenly she had a brainstorm. The football game. She could do one drawing of the players, one of the cheerleaders, and one of the spectators. With all the action in those scenes, it could be really exciting. There'd be a lot of contrast among the three pictures. And they'd certainly be relevant to life at New Falls High.

Charged by her idea, Joanne quickly finished a brief sketch of the football team involved in a complicated play.

As she began the next drawing, the cheerleaders going through one of their routines, Ms. Statman came over to where she was sitting. "Nice, Joanne. There's a lot of movement in your lines. I can really feel the action of the moment."

"Thanks. This is pretty different for me. I'm used to doing mostly quiet landscapes."

"What made you decide to try something new?"

"Well," Joanne said, hesitating, "I need a challenge. And I guess life here makes me think of more energetic things."

"Excellent," Ms. Statman said. "That's the way an artist thinks about a new project. You've chosen a subject that has meaning for you and then thought about what quality the subject suggests."

Joanne smiled. "Now all I have to do is get it on paper."

"Right, and that may be harder than you think," Ms. Statman replied. "You'll be working not only with a fairly new medium, pen and ink, but with a different style, too. If you run into trouble, don't get frustrated. Talk to me. I'm sure that together we'll be able to work out any problems." Then she went on to the next student.

Joanne sketched diligently throughout the period. She was so engrossed in what she was doing that she didn't sneak even one peek at Tony. She worked mainly on the first drawing, gradually making clear exactly what the play was. She put the quarterback in the center of the page, about to throw a pass to one of his teammates. The others were grouped around the goal post, waiting for the ball. By the end of class, she had two versions she liked a lot. Now she'd have to see if she could translate one of them into pen and ink.

"What's *that* supposed to be?" came a harsh voice from behind her. It was Skye.

Can't this girl leave me in peace? Joanne wondered. But she said out loud, "Is there something wrong with my sketch?"

"It looks like a soccer match, not a football game," the willowy blond answered cruelly. "No self-respecting football team would ever set up a defense that way. Don't you have any sense of football strategy?"

"I—I guess not," Joanne answered sheepishly. She knew her face must be purple with embarrassment. Skye was talking loudly enough for everyone in the class to hear.

"That's the worst picture I've ever seen," Skye declared. "At least mine has the facts straight."

Joanne shot a glance at Tony. He was staring at the floor in embarrassment. Maybe he was sorry now that he'd been friendly to someone so obviously out of it. Maybe he thought he'd wasted his lecture about football on her. She gulped for a breath of air.

Joanne knew this was the time to tell Skye off, the way Rusty had suggested. But she just couldn't bring herself to say anything. She was letting Skye humiliate her all over again, and now it was her own fault.

At that moment the bell rang, and Skye strode dramatically out of the room. Joanne felt almost sick with shame. All she wanted to do was to fly straight back to Alaska and never show her face in class again. She was just about to crumple the offending drawing into a tiny ball when Ms. Statman rushed over to her.

"Don't you dare touch that," she ordered. "This is only a first sketch, Joanne. Look at the beautiful, flowing lines you've created. It's a good beginning."

"But Skye said—"

"No buts. You've just run into one of those problems I told you about. Keep this drawing for its artistic value, but go to the library and take out a book on football plays or get a friend to explain some to you. Artists often have to do research for projects. Really, it's not as hard as it sounds."

Joanne sighed. "But it's hopeless. I'll never understand football strategy the way Skye does."

"Maybe not," the teacher admitted. "But you can get a good idea of one play. And from that, you can draw a real work of art."

"All right," Joanne conceded. "I'll go to the library during study hall."

"Good girl. I knew you wouldn't give up. Oh, and, Joanne, I don't know anything about defensive strategy either. I guess neither of us is as well informed as Skye." Ms. Statman gave Joanne a wink before she left.

Joanne spent a lot of time that morning thinking about the incident in art class. Skye had made a fool of her in front of Tony again. The whole thing really put a damper on her spirits. And to make matters worse, Rusty was out sick with a cold that day, so she didn't even have any-one to discuss it with.

Joanne was not looking forward to lunch at all. The cafeteria, so busy and noisy, still didn't feel comfortable to her. Until that day she'd been spared the humiliation of eating alone, but now, with Rusty home, she'd have to do just that. So once again she'd be the friendless outsider. The whole situation made her want to cry.

She dawdled for as long as she could before going down for lunch. First she went to the girls' room and straightened her clothes, but that didn't take too long. Then she went up to her locker and went through the combination, ever so slowly. She decided to bring a book with her. She'd need it while she was eating lunch alone. Finally she headed for the cafeteria.

Joanne didn't see anyone she knew in the lunchroom, which suited her fine. She was feel-ing too low to have a good conversation. At least Skye wasn't there. Maybe the beautiful cheer-leader hadn't realized how much her comment would hurt, but that didn't stop Joanne from feeling absolutely terrible. She got in the food line and waited her turn.

When she was about halfway through the line, she felt a tap on her shoulder. She turned to find Tony's green eyes staring into hers. "Hi. I'm glad you made it," he said. "I've been waiting for you."

"For me?" Joanne gasped.

"Yes. I wanted to talk to you about this morning." His gaze didn't waver, but Joanne could tell he felt uncomfortable.

"OK," she said. "Just let me get some food." This morning was the last thing she wanted to talk about with Tony.

Once they were seated across from each other at a secluded table in the corner, Tony began to speak. "Well, for one thing, I'm sorry it happened," he said, referring to the incident in art class.

"Me, too," Joanne mumbled, looking down at her egg salad sandwich.

"And for another thing, I saw your drawings, and I thought they were very nicely done."

Joanne's head jerked up. "So did Ms. Statman, but that wasn't exactly the point Skye was making." She bit into her sandwich to emphasize what she had said.

"I know," Tony admitted. "I wanted to talk to you about that, too. Football's a complicated sport. Of course you wouldn't understand how it works after seeing only one game."

Joanne breathed a sigh of relief. Tony wasn't sorry he'd spent time at the football game with her. "I guess I didn't realize how specific the game plays are. I don't know. Maybe I should forget about doing football scenes and go back to Alaskan landscapes."

"No, don't do that," Tony said quickly. "You're in class to try new things. Besides, you can learn about football if you really want to. It's easy. I bet you could come up with some beautiful drawings."

"Look," Joanne said, putting down her sandwich. "I know you're trying to make me feel better, but I don't think it's going to work. My drawing wasn't any good. And Skye made a pretty nasty comment to me. I can't just ignore it."

"That's another thing." Tony cleared his throat nervously. "I wanted to ask you, well—see, Skye is different from how you think she is. On the outside, she's beautiful and seems sure of herself. But on the inside, she's just like all the rest of us, with doubts and insecurities and stuff."

"You can't mean you want me to do something for her!" Joanne exclaimed. She was really getting angry. Her appetite had disappeared, so she just played with her sandwich, breaking it into smaller and smaller pieces.

"No, it's nothing you can do for her except—I guess I'm asking you to try to understand her. She's been going through a lot of hard stuff lately, and she's been taking it out on everyone She really doesn't mean it."

Joanne was amazed. Skye had insulted her and now Tony was asking *her* to try to under stand. It was crazy. "Tony," she said slowly, " don't think I can do what you're asking. Sky hasn't apologized to me or anything. For all know, she'll do the same kind of thing tomor row. If Skye is having problems, I'm sorry. Bu she has no right to lay them all on me."

"I'm just trying to help Skye," Tony added, hi voice filled with despair. "She's really a very spe cial girl, but I guess I can't expect you to see tha right now." Then his eyes brightened, and hi face broke into a warm smile. "But, Joanne, like you a lot. So if you want to, I'd love to hel you with your art project. Let's get togethe sometime and discuss football plays."

Joanne was too confused by the conversatio to think straight. Tony seemed to care mor about Skye's feelings than about her own. Bu then he'd practically asked her for a date! True talking about football certainly wasn't the mos romantic thing Joanne could think of, but ther was something about the way Tony had sug gested it that made it sound like fun. "Well– sure," Joanne said.

"Great!" Tony answered enthusiastically

"How about Friday afternoon? We can make plans in art class."

"OK."

"Joanne, I'm glad we talked," Tony said, taking her hand and giving it a little squeeze. "And don't worry about Skye and her comments. She doesn't realize what she's saying." And with that, Tony dashed out of the cafeteria.

Wow, Joanne said to herself. *What should I make of all that?* The most important thing seemed to be that Tony really was interested in her. He liked her a lot, he'd said. When Joanne thought about that, she couldn't help but let a delighted giggle escape. And what was more, she sort of had a date with him!

But if he cared so much for Skye, maybe he really did want a girl like her. What did that mean? A great wardrobe, perfect taste, self-confidence, poise. Well, Joanne didn't think any of those things were bad. In fact, she wished she had them all, too. But then again, Skye was also self-centered and nasty. Joanne didn't want those traits. But wasn't that just what Rusty had suggested—copy Skye's good points but not the bad ones? It was beginning to make sense. Joanne was starting to see that Rusty was right. She did need a crash course in Southern California culture. *And if you're going to do it, you'd better do it fast*, she told herself. *Friday is only four days away. That doesn't leave much time!*

Chapter Seven

The first thing Joanne did after school that day was rush over to Rusty's house to recount the whole story of Skye's put-down and her confusing conversation with Tony. She really needed a second opinion as to what it all meant.

Rusty's mother let Joanne in and told her she could go up to Rusty's room. Joanne found Rusty lying in bed, the stereo blasting.

"Wow, am I glad you showed up!" her friend exclaimed. "I'm so bored I could absolutely scream."

"How are you feeling?" Joanne asked with concern. She took off her sweater and dropped comfortably onto the edge of the bed.

"Oh, this old cold is nothing. I had a little fever this morning, but I'll be fine tomorrow."

"Well, school was anything but boring today,"

Joanne said. "I sort of wish it had been." She launched into a heated account of what had happened. "So what do you think?" she finished. "I'm not even sure if it's good news or bad news."

"The part with Skye is definitely bad news," Rusty declared.

"You can say that again!"

"But the part with Tony sounds pretty good."

"You really think so?" Joanne said excitedly.

"Sure. He asked you for a date, and he even told you he likes you. But hold on and don't get too happy too soon. He may like you, but he cares about Skye, too. Maybe he was hinting that he wants a girl who's a lot like her. You may have your work cut out for you."

"I know. I've been thinking about that, too." Joanne took a deep breath for courage. "Rusty, I've decided to listen to the advice you gave me on Saturday about updating my image. I can't stay boring old Joanne Trask from Alaska forever."

"That's exactly it!" cried Rusty. "You're a neat person, Joanne. I know that. Now you have to show everyone else."

"I kept thinking at school that Tony wouldn't want to spend time with someone he couldn't talk to about things like music and sports."

"And you need a new image, too," Rusty went on. "If you're going to become an expert in pop culture, you've got to look the part."

"What's wrong with the way I look?" Joanne asked, looking down at her new clothes and feeling a little hurt.

"Oh, that outfit's fine," Rusty assured her. "But you need more than one. When I'm over this cold, we'll go shopping at the mall. And another thing, no one wears their hair in a braid like that."

"But you had braids the other day," Joanne retorted.

"Yeah, braids," said Rusty, emphasizing the *s*. "That's different than one braid. You need a new hairstyle."

"Oh, no," Joanne warned, grasping possessively at her hair. "I could never cut it. It's sort of my trademark."

"You don't have to cut it to do something creative with it," Rusty insisted. "Come on." She hopped out of bed and picked up her desk chair, which she carried to the bathroom. She placed it in front of the full-length bathroom mirror and motioned for Joanne to sit down. "Welcome to Madame Rusty's Exotic Hair Salon," she said. "Madame Rusty awaits you."

"Is that a threat or a promise?" Joanne asked, taking her place before the mirror.

"Maybe a little of both." Rusty gathered together a comb and brush and an assortment of barrettes, combs, rubber bands, and hair bands. Then she gently unbraided Joanne's hair and brushed it. "Wow," she exclaimed when Joanne's wavy brown hair flowed free. "Your hair is great! It's absolutely a sin to keep this beautiful stuff hidden away in a braid all the time. Stupid, too. Any guy would flip over hair like this."

"Your compliments are beginning to sound an awful lot like insults," Joanne said dryly. But she knew her hair was pretty special.

"It's a compliment, kiddo. I'm really amazed." She lifted up a lock and let it float back into place. "Now, watch what I do. This style lets your gorgeous hair hang loose, but it will also keep it out of your face." She took a thick portion of hair from either side of Joanne's face and clipped the two together in the back.

Joanne looked at the new style in the mirror and liked what she saw. Her hair was floating like a silken cloud around her shoulders. She felt like a fairy princess. She shook her head to see if the clip would hold. It did, and the hair stayed out of her eyes. Rusty was right again. This would be a perfect style for school. "This is great, Rusty," Joanne said happily. "Thanks a lot."

"Or you can keep it neat with a hair band," Rusty explained, carefully arranging one on her riend's head. "We can get a few in different colors at the mall."

After that Rusty created a variety of hairstyles, using an off-center ponytail or braiding some of the hair and leaving the rest loose. Joanne especially liked the way she looked when Rusty parted her hair on the side, made three tiny braids, and left the rest loose.

"Really, Joanne, with hair like this, I can't believe you haven't experimented," Rusty scolded. "You can do anything with it. But enough about hairstyles. Now it's time for your music lesson."

Joanne followed Rusty back to the bedroom. Rusty knelt in front of a box of albums, flipped through them, and removed about ten. Then she went to her bookshelf and picked out a few books.

"We'll start with my favorites," she said. "The Space Pirates."

Joanne settled comfortably on the carpet. "Great. I've heard of them, and I always wondered what they sounded like."

"Joanne," Rusty groaned. "I just can't believe the neat things you people up in Alaska miss out on!" She removed an old record from the turntable and put the new one on. "Here," she said, throwing the album cover to Joanne. "This is what they look like. Don't you think Darwin is the cutest guy you've ever seen?"

"Which one is he?"

"The one in the middle. Here's a book about the Pirates with more pictures." She placed the needle on the record, and music flooded the room.

Joanne liked what she heard. The music had power, but there was an underlying smoothness to it. In the next hour she heard music by all of Rusty's favorite bands, most of them local to L.A. She and Rusty even danced to a few of the songs.

"Well, what do you think?" Rusty asked as the last strains of an Ex-Zombies tune faded away.

"For the most part, I like it."

"Good. Now, you told me you've never seen MTV. This is your chance." The girls went downstairs to the game room, and Rusty flicked on the television, then turned to the right channel. "Make yourself comfortable, and I'll go get us some soda and munchies."

Joanne had watched a few videos before Rusty came back. "This is fun," she called to her friend in the kitchen. "But it's a little like one long jeans commercial."

Rusty came back carrying two glasses and a bowl of chips on a tray. "Some of the videos are better than others," she said, placing the food on the floor next to Joanne. Then she sat down beside her to watch.

As it turned out, MTV was Joanne's least favorite of the day's lessons in pop. The videos were exciting at first, but they got repetitive after a while. And she and Rusty did a lot more talking and giggling when they had played with hairstyles and listened to albums. Sitting in front of the TV wasn't Joanne's idea of a fun afternoon. But she didn't tell Rusty that.

Finally Rusty flipped off the TV, and the girls went back up to her room. When they were settled comfortably on the bed, Rusty said, "So, you already look a lot different with your new clothes and new hairstyle. But you don't act differently. Skye's been bugging you ever since you first came to New Falls High, and you've just let her keep on doing it." Rusty looked at Joanne seriously. "Today sounds like it was a really bad scene."

"What do you think I should have done?" Joanne asked.

"Stuck up for yourself," Rusty said, hitting the bed with her palm for emphasis. "Don't let her walk all over you. You have to learn to be a little tougher. You've got to realize when to show your soft side and when to keep it hidden."

"How about giving me an example?" Joanne

toyed thoughtfully with the end of one of her three braids.

"OK, well, when I first came to New Falls, there was this girl who used to love to pick on me. Kind of the way Skye picks on you, but worse. Every time she'd say something mean to me, I'd start crying and run off to the bathroom. She knew she could get a rise out of me, so she picked on me even more."

"How did it all end?" Joanne asked.

"I finally stopped getting so upset, or at least showing that I was upset. Once she couldn't get a reaction out of me, the game wasn't fun anymore, and she quit bothering me."

"All right," Joanne said. "But I don't start crying when Skye says something mean to me."

"Of course not. But if she thought you had a little toughness in you, she'd probably leave you alone."

"You know, Rusty, I bet that's true. I'm an easy target."

"Right."

"So how do I use these ideas to help me out?"

"In a million ways," Rusty said, reaching for a tissue and blowing her nose. "Take this guy at school, Jamie, who I really like. I just don't come out and let him know how I feel, or he'd never get interested in me."

"Why?" That didn't make much sense to Joanne.

"I don't know. Boys are like that. It happened to me before with another guy. I scared him away, so now I don't want to be too obvious about my feelings." She turned on the radio with a click. "Anyway, that's all ancient history. Right now, the important thing is not to let Skye tromp all over you. You have to protect yourself. Think of clever ways to answer her back. And definitely don't let her or anyone else know how much her comments hurt you. That will blow your image in an instant."

"So what would you have done in the situation I was in today?" Joanne asked.

"Well, one thing would have been to cut her drawing down as much as she cut yours down."

"But then I'd be as bad as she is!" Joanne insisted.

"Huh-uh," Rusty said, shaking her head. "Because she started it. It's like she threw the first punch in a fistfight. No one would blame you for defending yourself."

Joanne knew she didn't want to be in a fistfight or the emotional equivalent of one. The truth was that Rusty's method of handling Skye really bothered her. She was feeling confused, but there was one thing she was sure of—she couldn't take any more of Skye's vicious taunting. So maybe she'd just have to put her reservations aside and give it a chance. She didn't know what else she could do. "You said that was one way. What would be another?"

"You could let her know what a creep you think she's being. That would probably get to her."

"But, Rusty—"

"I know it sounds a little mean," Rusty said gently. "But Skye probably won't leave you alone until you do something like that. I'm only trying to help you."

"OK, you may be right. But I still don't understand what all this has to do with you and Jamie."

"Well, I guess it's all a matter of not showing your weaknesses. I don't let Jamie know he makes my stomach do somersaults, and you shouldn't let Skye know she makes yours fall down to your feet."

"But if Jamie's a nice guy, which he probably is since you like him, why should you play games with him?"

"I got hurt once before," Rusty answered softly. "And I don't want to get hurt again. Anyway," she added, her voice stronger, "you do agree that it doesn't make sense to show your weaknesses to Skye, right?"

"Yes," Joanne admitted. "But even so, I don't

know if I can be nasty to her in the way you say I should be. I'll have to think about it."

Rusty nodded. "When you do that, you'll find out that I'm right."

"Maybe," Joanne replied, but she still didn't think she could react so harshly to anyone. It just wasn't her style.

The two girls sat quietly for a moment, each lost in her own thoughts, while a tender ballad played on the radio. Joanne thought about the past few weeks since she'd left Scranton. So much had happened that it felt much longer than that. She'd made a new best friend and possibly a new enemy. She'd had her first serious art lessons, and she'd met a guy she really liked. But most important she'd left her small town behind.

"You know," Joanne said, breaking the silence, "I'm sort of homesick for Scranton. It may be just a little town, but new kids don't get picked on there, so they don't have to put on a tough act to survive. California is just too different."

"And that's just it," Rusty shot back. "You're trying to pretend it isn't! You like all of New Falls's good points, but you refuse to accept its bad ones. Life isn't perfect here, Joanne, but it can be lots of fun if you adjust to it."

"Well, life in Scranton isn't perfect, either. I

guess I wouldn't be here if it were. Anyway, I'm here now, so I'll have to make the best of it."

"That's right. And if you want to make friends and not be an outsider, you're going to have to act like a California kid," Rusty exclaimed.

The walk home from Rusty's house gave Joanne a chance to go over the day's events in her mind. Skye, Rusty, Tony—the three conversations were all connected somehow. One thing she knew for sure was that she did want to make friends. So if Rusty thought a tough act was the way to do it, she'd act tough. Understand it or not.

Chapter Eight

Joanne's nervousness about her date with Tony disappeared after the first ten minutes with him. His ready smile and easygoing manner completely relaxed her. They had decided to meet at the library so they could look at books on football strategy. Tony had brought pads along to sketch the plays for Joanne as he explained various game plans. They settled themselves in a deserted corner so that their talking wouldn't disturb anyone.

"So what do you think?" Tony asked at last, pushing aside a pile of papers covered with diagrams of plays.

"I think I'm never going to understand this game," Joanne said and laughed. To herself she added, *But I don't mind as long as I've got you around to explain it to me.*

"Possibly," Tony conceded. "But you need only one play for your drawing. This one here, for instance." He picked up one of the diagrams. "It's not too complicated, and there's a lot of action in it."

"I like that one, too," Joanne agreed. She took the paper from Tony, folded it, and slipped it into her purse. "You know," she said, "I want to thank you for taking the time to help me with this project. I'm getting excited about it. I really think I can do a good sketch now."

"It was my pleasure," Tony answered. "And I mean that. To tell you the truth, I'm glad we got a chance to spend some time alone. Football games and art classes aren't too private."

Joanne looked at Tony for a moment. It was like a dream come true. This handsome, sensitive boy liked her. And she liked him. "I'm glad you asked me," she said shyly.

"Good. And now that we've finished our work, let's go out for a bite to eat. How about the Sea Shack? They've got the best fried clams in town."

"Sounds great," Joanne said. Actually, anything Tony might have suggested would have been fine with her. Just being with him was fantastic. *Wait until I write Maya about this! And Rusty will just die.*

"This is the place," Tony said, pulling up outside a small restaurant.

"Looks nice," Joanne remarked, stepping out of the car.

As they waited for their order of fried clams, Joanne and Tony talked about school and about their tastes in art. They discovered that they both loved impressionism but weren't too crazy about abstract paintings or sculptures.

Joanne couldn't believe how comfortable she felt with Tony—the way she would have with her friends in Scranton. But it was different, too. No one back home could relate to her about art the way Tony could. And, of course, no one made her feel so deliciously romantic.

Joanne was feeling terrific. It looked as though things just might work out for her in New Falls. In Tony she had a wonderful new friend and the possibility for romance. And almost as important, he had helped her work out the problem with her drawing.

The waitress arrived, setting a heaping plate of fried clams between Tony and Joanne. Joanne took one, dipped it into the sauce, and popped it into her mouth.

"What do you think?" Tony asked, also reaching for a clam.

"Good and crunchy," she said, considering the morsel in her mouth. "Nice flavor, but not nearly as nice as you," she finished boldly. "Tony, thanks again for showing me those football plays. They're really going to help me."

"As I said, it was my pleasure."

"You've saved me from a fate worse than death—drawing football games that look like soccer matches," Joanne said, joking.

But Tony didn't take Joanne's words lightly. He frowned and looked troubled. "Joanne, about Skye. I—I'm sorry for what she said to you."

"Why should *you* be sorry? Skye sure didn't seem as though she was," Joanne said truthfully, a hard edge creeping into her tone. She wished Tony would stop excusing Skye's cruel behavior.

"Joanne, I just wish you'd try to understand Skye. She's so fragile now. She really needs—"

But Joanne didn't let Tony finish. "Tony, I'm tired of hearing about what Skye needs," she cried in exasperation. "I have needs, too, and Skye sure isn't trying to understand them. My friend Rusty thinks I should stand up to her instead of being so calm and understanding all the time. And I'm beginning to agree with her."

"Oh, yeah, Rusty. I don't know why you hooked up with her," Tony retorted. "She and her friends walk around with chips on their shoulders."

"At least they're nice to new kids," Joanne shot back heatedly.

"But they're not particularly nice to anyone else," Tony returned, his face reddening.

"Hey, Tony, I don't get you," Joanne said, trying to calm down at least a little. "How can you be so understanding about Skye and so hard on everyone else?"

"Skye's got certain special problems—"

Joanne felt her anger rising again. And this time, instead of pushing it back politely, she let it out in a rush of words. It was almost as if she were taking her anger at Skye out on Tony. "Oh, I know Skye's got problems. Big problems. She's an insensitive bully, and she deserves to be put in her place," Joanne declared hotly.

"Great, so your friend Rusty thinks the best way to deal with that is to be an even bigger bully?"

"Maybe that's better than getting stepped on every time Skye is in a bad mood. Or having someone I thought I liked stick up for Skye no matter how mean she is to me."

Tony looked at Joanne for a moment as if he were digesting her words carefully. "Joanne," he said quietly. "Joanne, I'm sorry."

But Joanne was on an unstoppable roll. She'd finally let all her hurt and anger out, and she wasn't about to push it all back now. "Sorry is easy to say, Tony. You said it for Skye, and now you're saying it for yourself. But to tell you the truth, I'm pretty tired of hearing those words when nothing really changes. If you think Skye is so wonderful, why don't you find someone just like her? And that means someone other than me!"

The minute the words were out of her mouth, Joanne couldn't believe she'd said them. Her first instinct was to take them back. But, in his own way, Tony had been just as insensitive as Skye.

Joanne pulled her sweater off the back of her chair. Then she stood up and turned to leave.

"Joanne—"

Joanne whirled around to face Tony one more time. There was a forlorn look in his eyes. Joanne knew he only had to say one word to her, and she'd forgive him completely. She'd sit back down and finish the plate of clams as if there'd been no argument at all.

"Joanne, I'm sorry it turned out this way," Tony said, his gaze dropping to the floor.

Joanne looked at Tony for one long moment, then turned and walked slowly out the door.

Chapter Nine

"Watch out, world, here comes Joanne Trask!" Rusty cried as she and Joanne caught sight of the New Falls mall. They had just crested one of the hills the kids used as a shortcut to get to the mall.

Joanne gave her friend a quick hug and giggled. "With her fabulous new hairstyle by Madame Rusty." She began to applaud loudly.

"Thank you, thank you," Rusty said, bowing to Joanne. "But wait until you see what Madame Rusty can do with your clothes. Come on, let's hit the mall."

The girls ran down the hill. It was another perfect California Saturday, the sun shining bright in a cloudless sky. Joanne breathed in the fresh, crisp air, happy that she had asked Rusty to go shopping with her. She still felt badly about the scene with Tony the day before, but she wasn't going to let that spoil this glorious day.

"The first thing we have to do is buy you the basics of a wardrobe," Rusty declared as they reached the entrance to the mall. "And there's no better place for that than Abondanza's."

"What's that?"

"The best little boutique around. They've got everything you need and at reasonable prices."

"Great," Joanne said. "My grandparents said they'd buy some clothes for me, but I think I'd like to use some of the money I saved working at the Tundra."

The girls entered the mall, and Rusty led Joanne to a completely different section than her grandmother had. It was decorated to look like a big city, with flashing neon signs and painted skyscrapers.

"This is it," Rusty said, turning into a store with mirrored walls and shag carpeting. Top-40 music blared through speakers, and brightly colored clothes were packed closely together on circular racks.

Joanne looked around in amazement. "You're going to have to tell me where to begin. I'm overwhelmed!"

"Great! I love picking out clothes, even if they're not for me. Now, the first thing you need are some shirts."

By the time Rusty had gone through two racks of blouses and a pile of T-shirts, she had about ten shirts for Joanne to try on. "You're only allowed to take three items into the dressing room at a time," she explained. "So you go in there, and I'll feed you shirts as you finish with them."

Out of the ten, Joanne chose two blouses, one in a pink-and-white geometric print and one a bright purple, and three T-shirts—a yellow one, a black one with a low back, and one purposely spattered with gray paint. Then Rusty went on to get Joanne baggy cotton sweaters to go with a plaid, knee-length skirt, a casual black dress with a fitted waist, and a pair of gray cotton pants.

"That's enough for today. All this stuff is good for school. If you have to go someplace fancy, we'll come back and get you a dynamite dress. But we don't want to make you or your grandparents broke all in one shopping spree."

"Fantastic!" Joanne cried. "I love the way these clothes look on me, and if I mix and match the tops and bottoms, I'll have about a dozen different outfits here."

"That's the way to do it," Rusty said. "Now, the most important part of an outfit is the accessories. The right belt or scarf can make or break the way you look." She walked over to a display and chose a red studded belt and three silk scarves. "Perfect," she declared, smiling with satisfaction. "And one more thing you definitely need," she added. "Sunglasses! Here, try these on."

After leaving the boutique, Rusty's next stop was the video arcade. Joanne had never seen anything like it. At least thirty gleaming machines stood against the walls, all bleeping and shrieking at the same time. The room reverberated with weird electronic sounds.

Contrary to what Joanne had expected, the video arcade was filled with all ages and types of people. In addition to the preps, jocks, valley types, and punks, all of whom obviously went to New Falls High, there were younger kids, probably in junior high or below. There were also several businessmen dressed in conservative three-piece suits taking their turns at the machines. Their attaché cases were at their feet. "They come in here for a few quick games," Rusty whispered. Joanne also saw a woman with a baby stroller and a grandmotherly type, both eagerly punching away at the games.

"Wow, this place is neat!" Joanne laughed.

"Oh, it's all right, I guess," Rusty drawled, her tone very different from what it had been moments earlier.

"What do you mean? You were raving over this

arcade on the way over. Now you say—" Joanne took a good look at her friend. Rusty's whole attitude had suddenly changed. Something about the way she was standing and the bored look on her face. It was a character Rusty sometimes put on in the cafeteria when she felt uncomfortable.

"See that guy over there playing Millipede?" Rusty hissed, pointing to a tall boy with blond hair. "That's Jamie."

"Ohhh," Joanne said, suddenly realizing what was going on.

The boy finished his game and, glancing up, spotted Rusty, who pretended to be looking everywhere except at him. He walked over to the girls. "Hi, Rusty, how's it going?" he asked, giving her a big smile.

Rusty looked as if she'd just noticed him. "Oh, hi, Jamie," she said nonchalantly.

"You here for a few games?"

"I guess you could say that. My friend Joanne just moved to New Falls, so I'm showing her around." Rusty's tone seemed to say that she had better places to be than a silly video arcade.

"I just had a really great game on Millipede," Jamie said. "I almost beat Ralph Lipito's high score."

"You did?" Rusty exclaimed excitedly. Then she realized that her response didn't fit in with her "who cares" style. "I mean, I hear Ralph is

OK at that game. Well, I've got a lot more places to show Joanne."

"Oh," Jamie said, sounding a little disappointed. "Um, well, I'm glad we ran into each other."

"Uh-huh," Rusty replied. "Well, bye." She sauntered out of the arcade, leaving Joanne to follow her.

Once outside the arcade in the mall's urban-style street, Joanne grabbed Rusty's hand and spun her around to face her. "Why did we leave so fast?" she wanted to know. "I think Jamie really liked talking to you. And I didn't even get to try any of the games."

"There's another arcade around here. We can go play at that one."

"But why did we leave this one, especially when Jamie was there? You like him! Don't you want to spend time with him?"

"Joanne, you don't understand yet. It's better my way. I know it is."

Joanne heaved a deep sigh. With a nice guy like Jamie, she didn't see how it possibly could be.

The other arcade was not so nice as the first one. It was smaller, and the decor was kind of shabby. Joanne tried a few of the games. She wasn't very good at them, but they were fun to play anyway. Still, she was a little upset about the way Rusty had treated Jamie, and it took some of the fun out of the afternoon.

"Listen, Joanne, let's get out of here and go get some pizza. I'm starved," Rusty said after they'd finished.

"You know," Joanne said sheepishly, "I've always wondered what the real stuff tastes like."

"What?" Rusty cried in disbelief. "You've never eaten pizza?"

"Just the frozen kind," Joanne said. "It never tastes as good as it looks in the TV commercials."

"You," Rusty declared with a shake of her head, "are a deprived child. It is cruel and unusual punishment to condemn a nice girl like you to eating only frozen pizza. Why, real pizza is as American as apple pie and baseball."

"Base what?" Joanne asked, keeping a straight face.

"No!" Rusty shrieked. "That's too much. You must have heard of baseball. Tell me you're joking, please."

"Of course I am." Joanne laughed. "I swear, Rusty, you're almost as gullible as I am."

"Well, let's get going. The sooner you sink your teeth into Rocco's light crust, the sooner you're on your way to understanding the California mind. After all, you are what you eat, and we eat a lot of Rocco's pizza around here."

Rocco's was a small place, nothing fancy, with

a few wooden tables and a long counter facing the pizza ovens. Joanne watched in fascination as the man behind the counter threw the round pizza dough in the air and caught it. She couldn't help but think of Tony. What would a boy who saw football as a kind of ballet think of this graceful chef? The man sent the dough sailing toward the ceiling once again with a smooth flip of his hand.

"What if he misses?" Joanne asked.

"He never does."

The girls ordered slices with everything on them. After all, Rusty reasoned, Joanne's first real pizza ought to be the best. Then they found a table and sat down to wait for their food.

"Joanne," Rusty said, "I'm proud to be the person who introduces you to Rocco's pizza, the most popular food in New Falls."

"This may sound weird to a veteran pizza eater like you," Joanne asked, "but *why* is it so great?"

"For one thing," Rusty answered, "eating pizza is very messy, and that's fun! But just wait until you taste it. You won't need another word of explanation."

When the pizza arrived, Joanne certainly did her share of oohing and ahhing—especially on the first bite, when she burned the roof of her mouth. "Worth it," she declared through a mouthful of cheese.

The girls rushed home after their snack at Rocco's because it was getting late. As she jogged home, her stomach full of pizza, her arms full of packages, Joanne decided it had been a perfect outing.

Chapter Ten

Joanne walked into art class on Monday feeling very stylish in her new clothes. She didn't look forward to seeing Tony again, but since she had to, she felt she ought to look her best. As she pushed the door open, she saw Tony glance at her, then quickly turn his head away. She swallowed a lump of disappointment and stepped through the doorway, her head held high.

But then Joanne heard Skye's harsh voice behind her. "Very nice outfit, but what happened to the Nanook of the North wardrobe you've been wearing?" Skye said it just loud enough for everyone in the room to hear.

Oh, no! Joanne thought. *Why does she have to start in on me first thing?* She glanced around the room for a friendly face. Tony was staring at the ground angrily. Joanne sighed. *Well, she* decided, *if you're going to try out Rusty's advice, there's no time like the present. You've got nothing to lose, anyway.*

She turned to Skye and stared directly into her eyes. "Are you referring to the Inuit of the Arctic? Some very ignorant people call them the Nanooks."

"What kind of people?" Skye asked in disbelief. "Are you calling me ignorant?"

"Yes, I am," Joanne answered coolly. "There's a lot you don't know." Then she turned and walked calmly to her easel without a backward glance.

Joanne's heart was racing. *You did it!* she thought excitedly. *You did just what Rusty wanted you to do.* She had stood up for herself. She hadn't let Skye get away with one more nasty comment.

Joanne glanced around the room to see what kind of reaction she had caused. Some of the kids were whispering as they looked at her or Skye. Others were purposely looking away from them both, as if they were embarrassed by the whole incident.

But Skye's face was the most surprising. She was beet red and was staring down at her notebook as if it were the most interesting thing in the world. She looked as if she wanted to melt into the linoleum floor. Joanne never thought she'd see Skye like that.

All of a sudden Joanne didn't feel so thrilled about having put Skye down. She'd been just as rude and insensitive as Skye had been. That was just what her grandmother and Tony had warned her about. But then, Skye had had it coming to her, didn't she? She'd pushed Joanne again and again. She deserved a taste of her own medicine.

Joanne's thoughts were interrupted when Ms. Statman walked into the room and started class. That day's lecture was on artistic composition, a subject Joanne usually would have found fascinating. But right then, her mind couldn't concentrate on her teacher's words; it kept wandering back to Skye.

She wondered why Skye had chosen to pick on her. Joanne had never done anything to annoy her. In fact, she'd truly wanted to be friends with Skye at first. It was Skye who had really blown that possibility by treating Joanne so badly.

All through class, Joanne's feelings kept flipping back and forth. First she'd think that she'd been right to act as she did, and then she'd think that she'd been wrong. By the end of the period, she was ready to tear her hair out from changing her mind so many times. She hadn't heard a word of Ms. Statman's lecture, and the new sketches she'd done during the second half of class weren't any good at all. She struggled to give the figures she was drawing some grace and beauty. But she struggled even more to make sense out of the disturbing incident with Skye.

Soon the bell rang, and everyone was gathering up books, art supplies, and drawings. Joanne glanced up to find Ms. Statman beckoning for her to come over to her desk.

Joanne walked over to her teacher. "Did you want something, Ms. Statman?" she asked.

"Yes, Joanne," Ms. Statman said. "Tell me, are you having any problems?" For a moment Joanne thought she meant the thing with Skye. "You know," the teacher went on, "any problems with your artwork?"

"Well—" Joanne hesitated. She was still having trouble with her drawings of the football game, but she was reluctant to talk about it with her teacher. Even after the session on plays with Tony, the sketches just weren't coming out right. They seemed lifeless, in spite of all the action. And Joanne knew it.

"Joanne, as I've said before, you have a special artistic touch. I can see it in the landscapes of Alaska you brought in to show me. But that touch isn't coming through in the football series. I think we both see that."

"You're right," Joanne said, hanging her

head. "But I don't know what's wrong." She was holding back tears. This conversation, on top of all her confusion about Skye and Tony, was hard to take.

"Now, don't get so upset," the teacher urged, resting her hand comfortingly on Joanne's bowed shoulder. "I didn't say the pictures never would work, just that they don't now. So we have to figure out why, together."

"OK," Joanne said. "I promise I'll do my best."

"I know you will. So let's both think about this and discuss it in a few days. Now, you'd better get going, or you'll be late to your next class."

Joanne put away her art materials, picked up her bag, then hurried into the hall. What a horrible class that had been. Everything that could have gone wrong had. All Joanne could hope was that the day would improve from there.

But that was not to be. She walked into the cafeteria, dreading the lunch period. She never really felt at ease there. It was too crowded and noisy, and she could never concentrate on her conversations.

Joanne found Rusty sitting at a table with a few of her friends. "So," Rusty said as Joanne took a seat, placing her lunch tray carefully on the table. "Remember when I told you about the Ex-Zombies concert?"

"Sure," Joanne replied, opening a carton of

milk and unwrapping a cheese and tomato sandwich.

"Well, the tickets are going on sale tomorrow, and Andy is going to go down to get us some." Rusty nodded toward Andy, a blond boy with a flat-topped haircut and a faded Clash T-shirt. "You still want to come, right?"

"Definitely," Joanne mumbled, her mouth full of sandwich. She sure wasn't going to pass up her first rock concert.

"Great," said Andy. "You're going to love the band. Their concerts are really dynamite."

"Yeah," added Sharon, a girl at the table. "We're real fans of the Ex-Zombies."

"We sure are," a dark-haired girl named Rosa said. "We haven't missed a concert they've done within fifty miles of L.A."

The conversation continued about the Ex-Zombies, then moved on to music in general, classes, teachers, and friends. And for once Joanne felt included. And that felt good.

Still, something nagged at her. It seemed as though Rusty's group was much more interested in her now that she had on stylish clothes. Why did a skirt and belt matter so much? Wasn't she the same Joanne no matter what clothes she wore?

Another thing that bothered her was the way these kids always talked about "we." They rarely

said, "I like that," but expressed their prefer-
ences by speaking for the whole group—"We like
that." *What's going on?* Joanne wondered. *Don't
they think for themselves?*

But in spite of all that, it was fantastic to be
part of a lively and warm group. It was the first
time that she hadn't felt like an outsider, and
she wasn't about to knock her new friends or the
comfortable niche she'd found for herself with
them.

"You know," Andy was saying, "last time I
went to get Ex-Zombies tickets, it was a real
drag. The lines were incredibly long, and there
were some very pushy people there."

"Hey," said Sharon, "it just means that the
band is finally getting some recognition."

"Yeah, but I had two people try to cut in front
of me."

"What did you do?" Joanne asked.

"I sent them to the back of the line, of course,"
he replied. "No one was going to push me
around. No one."

"You know, something kind of like that happened to me in art class today," Joanne told the
group, deciding to confide in them. She needed
to get the whole thing about Skye off her chest
anyway. She went through the story quickly,
without mentioning how badly she felt afterward.

"Neat, Joanne" was Rusty's response. "I knew you could do it."

"Way to go," said Nic, a curly-haired boy. "Skye needed it. She's a real snob." The general consensus was that Joanne had done a really fantastic thing by standing up to Skye.

"I can't imagine her looking hassled," a slim girl named Diane remarked.

"Neither could I," Joanne admitted, and she found herself telling the group about her mixed-up feelings after the scene.

"But she started it," said Rusty.

"Yeah, she asked for it," agreed Sharon.

Joanne took a deep breath. *Right*. She'd thought of those excuses, too. But, somehow, they just didn't satisfy her. Still, she wasn't about to tell that to Rusty and the others.

Joanne glanced over at Rusty and smiled. What a great person. Without her advice and help, without her friendship, Joanne would be another loner, sitting by herself with a cheese sandwich for company. There were certainly enough of those kids at New Falls High, kids who didn't fit into any one group and got lost in the shuffle. Joanne was glad she wasn't one of them. She belonged. She had the style.

So, if her friends liked her new taste in clothes, that's what Joanne would wear. And if they got a kick out of her telling Skye off, she'd continue to do so. Joanne pushed back the thoughts about losing Tony. *Forget him*, she told herself firmly. *This is the social life I want.*

The bell sounded for the end of lunch, and everyone took off for class, amid choruses of goodbyes.

Chapter Eleven

"The movie was great," Joanne said, blinking groggily as she, Rusty, and a few of the other girls from the gang emerged into the sunlight. It was another beautiful Saturday. "Now where to?" she asked.

"Let's go over to Burgerland and have a couple of burgers," Diane suggested.

"Sounds good," Sharon said, and the others agreed, too.

"So what did you think of the movie?" Rosa asked once they were seated at a booth.

"Pretty good," answered Diane.

Sharon grimaced, clearly disagreeing. "The ending was sappy. I mean, I'm getting a little tired of these romantic wrap-ups."

Joanne looked at Sharon in surprise. How could she say that? Joanne had heard Sharon sniffling all through the last part of the film. Rusty, who had been sitting on Sharon's other side during the movie, glanced at Joanne and winked. So she knew, too.

"I liked the ending," Diane admitted. "It was kind of bittersweet."

The waiter came over, and they all ordered burgers, except Rosa, who was a vegetarian. She ordered a bowl of vegetarian chili and a salad.

"But it wasn't very realistic," insisted Sharon. "Those storybook endings don't really exist."

"What do you mean?" Joanne asked. To her the movie had been a simple, sweet romance, just the kind she loved. Pushing through obstacle after obstacle, the girl and boy had finally come together because their love was so strong. Was that so unrealistic?

"Well," Sharon answered, "how many of us have ever had a boyfriend that considerate and devoted? I don't think there *are* boys like that."

Rusty nodded in agreement. "She's got a point there. I really cared about my last boyfriend, but he couldn't even wait through one summer for me."

"That's right," Sharon said. "The boy in the movie was too good to be true."

"Oh, come on, Sharon," said Rosa. "Andy is pretty sensitive to you."

"True," Sharon admitted, "but we've only been

seeing each other for three weeks so far. I *hope* he's like the guy in the movie, but I'm definitely not counting on it."

"I don't know," Diane mused. "I guess I'm more of a romantic than you are."

Joanne smiled. She liked Diane.

"I feel somewhere between the two of you," Rusty said. "I'm pretty sure I'll find a neat guy, but I figure I'll have to meet a bunch of rotten ones first." She laughed. "Of course, if I had my wish, Jamie would turn out to be the boy of my dreams."

"So, Joanne, are you interested in someone around here?" Rosa wanted to know. "Or did you leave your true love behind in Alaska?"

Joanne blushed. Even though she had told herself to forget Tony, she couldn't stop thinking about him. To say the least, things hadn't been going too well between them since the day at the restaurant. He had consistently avoided her. So if nothing was happening between them right now, why even talk about him?

"There was a guy named Danny at home, but he wasn't anyone really special," she said lightly. "I mean, he was special, but not as a serious boyfriend, so I'm a free agent. But I'm not looking for anyone here, either. Boys!" she groaned. "Who needs them?" The other girls laughed, and

Joanne knew she'd said the right thing, even though it wasn't at all true.

The conversation continued with the girls relating stories about different boys they had gone out with. Rusty and Sharon joined in, mostly complaining about how boys were more trouble than they were worth. Joanne didn't agree with them, but she didn't tell them that. She wanted romance. She loved imagining scenes that might occur between her and Tony, things they would do together, secrets they would share.

She was glad when the conversation turned to the Ex-Zombies concert. When they were talking about boys, Joanne felt everyone was trying to impress the others with their "I-don't-care" attitudes. Joanne really liked the girls, but she hated how much they stretched the truth.

After they'd finished eating, the girls went to the arcade to play a few games. The arcade was packed, but Rusty managed to get two good machines next to each other, which they all took turns playing in pairs. Because there were five of them, one girl was always waiting her turn. Joanne watched first, trying to figure out the best strategies for the games by studying how the others played. When her turn came, she did pretty well.

"Can you believe that score?" Rosa exclaimed.

"This girl had never seen a video game until last month."

"Not true," Joanne said. "Even Scranton has one video machine now. That means they must be *everywhere*. It was an arcade I'd never seen, not a video game."

The girls kept feeding quarters into the machines and taking turns, so absorbed in their games that they didn't notice how crowded the place was getting. The group had ended up playing a kind of tournament, with Rusty and Sharon as high scorers. They were about to have a play-off when a short, chubby boy about seven came up to the machine they were still using and put his quarter on it.

"There are no other games free, and you guys have been playing for hours," the boy said. "How about giving the rest of us a chance?"

Sharon looked down at the boy and smiled. "We're just getting to the play-off of our tournament. So be patient and we'll be done soon." She got another quarter out of her pocket and pushed it into the game.

"Hey, are you going to play again?" the boy whined. "That's no fair. I put my quarter down."

"Look, kid, you can't always get what you want when you want it. I asked you to be patient. We're in the middle of something important."

"I've been waiting too, you know," the boy

cried. "You guys think you're so important. Well, I don't care about your dumb tournament."

"We're not guys," said Sharon, her eyes focused on the video screen.

Joanne watched the exchange with mounting alarm. The kid definitely had a point. They had played a lot, and there were plenty of other people waiting. And he *had* put his quarter down. Her friends were being selfish; the tournament really could wait. It also bothered her that Sharon was taking advantage of this little kid because she was older. As the boy said, it wasn't fair. But Joanne didn't know what to say or do about it, so she just kept quiet, feeling worse and worse by the minute.

Suddenly Joanne saw Tony. She had longed to see him, but right then she wished he were clear up in Alaska. She wasn't proud of what was going on, and of all people, she didn't want Tony to see it. But, of course, he did, along with half the people in the arcade.

"Typical," he said angrily. "As usual, the older kids are hogging the machines. It happens every time I'm in here."

There was a moment of awkward silence as the girls realized what they were doing. The silence stretched out uncomfortably. Joanne longed to shout out, "You're right, Tony. And we're sorry, truly sorry." She also wished she could change the unhappy frown on the chubby little boy's face into a smile. But she couldn't. If she did, she'd lose the only friends she had in New Falls. And they were nice girls; they just weren't all that considerate sometimes.

Suddenly Rusty broke the silence. "OK, the kid can play. He can even use our quarter. Come on, gang, let's get out of this place."

The girls filed out of the arcade, trying to save face after their little disaster. Joanne followed along, feeling clumsy and embarrassed. She could sense Tony's eyes boring into her back. He must think she was a real creep.

The group split up once they were outside. No one wanted to discuss the incident, so they quickly went their separate ways. Joanne had to be alone to think things over.

She walked swiftly toward a small park she had discovered the week before. She had been looking for a place to do some sketching and had stumbled upon Candle Garden. It was a pretty little spot filled with trees, shrubs, and beds of brightly colored flowers. Just picturing those gorgeous blossoms made Joanne feel a little better.

When she reached the park, Joanne strolled over to a stone bench, sat down, and sighed wearily. She was so mixed up. She definitely agreed with Rusty that she couldn't let people walk all over her. And she had shown Skye that she wouldn't put up with it and now the girl left her alone.

But, she'd made Skye feel rotten, and even if Skye was kind of rotten herself, it wasn't right.

Worst of all, though, this whole incident had gotten her into a useless, probably irreconcilable fight with Tony. It was true that he had acted badly, but Joanne had to admit that she had, too. If only she'd been a little more flexible and understanding with him!

She sighed and stood up. "I just don't know what's right anymore," she said out loud. Then she walked out of the garden toward home, more confused than ever.

Chapter Twelve

"That's what you're wearing to a concert?" Mrs. Trask asked in disbelief as Joanne walked into the living room in her black jeans and a black T-shirt. "It takes you an hour to get ready, and that's how you end up looking?"

"Grandma," Joanne said, "this is the way everybody is going to be dressed. I asked Rusty." She threw the black sweater she was carrying onto the couch and adjusted her red studded belt.

"But you have several nice skirts in your closet," Mrs. Trask persisted. "I see you wearing them to school all the time. Why do you want to look like a hit man tonight?"

"You don't understand," Joanne said defensively. "This is what you're supposed to wear to a rock concert."

Mrs. Trask smiled lovingly at her granddaughter. "Oh, I guess I do. We wore some crazy fashions when I was young, too. Sorry, Joanne. I overreacted." Mrs. Trask kissed Joanne on the forehead and handed her the black sweater.

"Oh, Grandma, I'm sorry I snapped at you. I guess I'm just worked up about this concert."

Mrs. Trask gave Joanne a quick hug. "Of course you are. Now run along and don't mind your old-fashioned grandmother."

"OK. Thanks, Grandma," Joanne said, opening the front door. "I'll try not to be too late."

Then Joanne ran all the way to Rusty's house, where the gang was meeting. She was on her way to her first rock concert, and she was so excited she thought she'd burst!

When Joanne rang the door bell, Rusty answered it. "Hi, come on in. Diane and Rosa are here already, but no one else is."

"Really? I thought I was late," Joanne said.

"Oh, rock shows never start on time. So we don't worry too much about getting there early."

Rusty led Joanne into the living room, where the others were sitting around drinking sodas. "Hey," Rosa greeted her. "You look like you're all ready for the show."

"I can't wait," Joanne said, taking a chair. "I've been hearing about the Ex-Zombies ever since I came from Alaska. If they're half as good in concert as they were on the record Rusty played for me, it's going to be a night to remember."

"It definitely will be that," agreed Diane.

Rosa passed Joanne a bowl of chips, then settled back on the sofa. "Diane was just telling me about her ballet class. She's getting so good, her teacher wants her to take more classes. Isn't that neat?"

Joanne turned to Diane in surprise. "Wow, I didn't know you're a dancer," she exclaimed.

"Well, sometimes I'm a little shy about telling people," Diane said.

"Joanne's an artist. Did she tell you that?" Rusty spoke up.

"Really?" said Diane. "I guess you're as shy about that as I am about dancing."

Joanne shook her head in amazement. "It's funny. There's a lot we don't know about one another. I guess I never really thought about what any of you do when you're not hanging out together at the mall."

"So how did you get into art?" Rosa wanted to know.

Joanne laughed. "At first it was just something to do on those long, cold winter afternoons in Alaska. But then I started liking it more and more. Now I don't think I could ever give it up."

"That's sort of like me and dancing," Diane

said. "I started because I have asthma and my doctor said dancing would strengthen my lungs. But then I began getting into it for its own sake."

"I can't believe we've known each other for almost two months, and we never mentioned these things," Joanne burst out, suddenly feeling much closer to Diane. They had more in common than just playing video games at the mall. "Do you have a hobby?" she asked, turning to Rosa.

"Not like you and Diane, but I do a lot of volunteering at the retirement center. And I help out at my parents' hardware store sometimes."

"Hey," Joanne said, "don't you think it's kind of crazy that we never said anything about these things? I mean, I was beginning to think that all California kids do is hang out and let themselves be entertained by video games and special TV channels."

"And I never could imagine what you did in Alaska for fun," Rosa said. "It *is* pretty weird."

The door bell rang, and Rusty jumped up to get it. "That must be Andy, Nic, and Sharon. They're driving over together."

As the three others came into the room, the energy level rose. Andy, Sharon, and Nic had definitely been psyching themselves up for the concert.

"Hey, gang," cried Andy. "Ready to rock 'n' roll?"

"Ex-Zombies, here we come!" yelled Sharon.

"So let's get going already," Diane said, jumping up from her chair. "We've been waiting for you guys for ages."

"All right," said Andy. "Sharon, Nic, and I will take my car. You four take Rusty's. We'll meet outside the Palace." The girls grabbed their sweaters, and everyone went outside and piled in the cars. Then they were on their way.

The talk, of course, was all about the Ex-Zombies—past shows, new songs, the new single. Joanne wished for a moment that they could have continued the conversation they'd been having at Rusty's, but then she got caught up in the mood, and it didn't seem to matter.

Joanne had seen the Palace Theatre from the outside, a huge building decorated with the art deco patterns of the 1930s. It had once been a fancy movie theater before it was converted into a rock concert hall. It was one of the oldest buildings in New Falls. Joanne had always wondered what it looked like on the inside. Now she'd get her chance to see.

Andy, Sharon, and Nic were waiting outside when the girls arrived. Andy handed tickets around, and then they all went in. The lobby of the Palace was painted with murals of people in

1930s clothes. Joanne liked the contrast between them and the kids who stood around waiting for the show to begin.

There were a lot of people dressed in jeans, like Joanne and her friends, but there were also kids in leather pants and miniskirts, ripped T-shirts, and really strange haircuts. At first Joanne felt a little threatened by them, but when a girl with pink and orange hair smiled at her, she began to relax. Everyone was just as excited about the show as she was!

The concert hall itself was really impressive. A huge crystal chandelier hung from the ceiling, and there were more art deco designs on the balconies. The stage was set up with gigantic speakers, electric instruments, and a massive drum set. Again Joanne noticed the contrast between the old and the new.

Joanne and her friends found their seats. Andy had been lucky enough to get really good ones—tenth row center. Soon the lights went out, and a guy in jeans and an Ex-Zombies T-shirt came out on the stage to announce the warm-up band, a group called the Dustbins.

They turned out to be pretty good. They had a gentle, soothing sound, using interesting harmonies. Joanne liked them, but she noticed that more people were talking than listening. "Too mellow," she heard a girl behind her say. "When are they going to crank up the sound and bring out the real music?"

The Dustbins played five or six songs, then thanked everyone in the house and left to scattered applause. That's when the energy level in the Palace really hit the roof. As the crew removed the Dustbins' equipment and replaced it with that of the Ex-Zombies, the audience began whistling, hooting, and calling out the names of the musicians in the band.

"All right," Rusty shouted to Joanne. With all the noise, yelling was the only way to communicate.

The announcer came on, and the yelling increased. "Ladies and gentlemen," he cried, "the Ex-Zombies!"

The crowd went wild as the band walked on the stage. There were three guys and two girls, all wearing white outfits. They went right into a song. The sound was clear, and the rhythm rocked.

Suddenly it seemed as though all the kids in the house were on their feet and moving madly to the beat. It didn't matter how well you danced. Joanne did take a peek over at Diane. Her ballet training showed. She was really graceful.

Joanne had always enjoyed dancing to records with her friends in Scranton. The concert was a lot like that, only much, much better. Joanne really felt comfortable here, even among hun dreds of strangers. She got Rusty's attentio and beamed a huge smile at her. "I knew you' like them," Rusty shouted.

Most of the songs were loud and fast, but ther was an occasional slow one thrown in. At on point the lead guitarist got out an acoustical gu tar and crooned a wistful ballad. Joanne, alon with the rest of the audience, listened wit unblinking attention.

When a fast song came on again, Joann danced with all her might, but then she began t feel tired. Even though she liked the music, i was hard to keep her energy level up. She sa down and really listened to the song. It had good, danceable rhythm with an interestin melody and poetic words. Pretty soon she was o her feet again, jumping and shaking to the com pelling sound of the Ex-Zombies.

At last came a really gorgeous song. The bea was so involving that Joanne knew no one in th world could ever sit still for it. It turned out to b the group's last. "Thank you very much," calle the lead vocalist, and the group bounded off th stage.

"Is that it?" Joanne asked Rusty, disap pointed that the show was over.

"No, they'll come back and do at least one mor song," Rusty told her.

The encore was obviously one of the fans' favorite songs. There was more dancing, and a lot of people sang along.

When the lights finally came up, it was a little bit of a letdown. What did you do after all that action?

For Joanne and her friends, the answer was to go to Rocco's Pizzeria at the mall. Over the food there was a lot of talk about the concert and not much else. At first Joanne joined in the lively conversation, but then she lost interest in going over and over the same thing.

Joanne toyed with the straw in her glass. What was wrong with her, anyway? Everything they'd done that evening had been fun. Then why did she feel so dissatisfied?

Suddenly it dawned on her what it was. Every time she got together with her friends, they went someplace to be entertained. Either they went and got food or went to the video arcade, a movie, or a concert. They never took walks, went for drives, or talked about their hopes and dreams for the future. Those were all things Joanne had enjoyed doing with her friends in Scranton.

The kids here were all so—so unimaginative. They saved their creative ideas, like dancing and volunteering, for themselves. But when they were together, they couldn't think of anything to do unless someone—or something—was amusing them. Joanne couldn't imagine how they'd survive in Scranton.

That night, as they were leaving Rocco's, Joanne took Diane aside. "Listen," she said, "I'd really like to come watch your dance class sometime if you wouldn't mind. I've never seen a ballet class. I'm kind of curious."

Diane looked surprised, then pleased. "Sure," she said. "I guess I never thought anyone would be interested in ballet except me. But if you want to come, I don't mind. In fact, I'd like it."

Joanne smiled to herself as she left. She was beginning to see that her Californian friends could learn a lot from her, maybe even as much as she learned from them!

Chapter Thirteen

The morning after the concert, Joanne woke up to a gray day, the first she had seen since coming to New Falls. That was fine with her—it matched her mood. She slipped on her bathrobe and shuffled groggily into the kitchen, where her grandfather was cooking breakfast.

"Good morning, Joanne. How was the concert?" he asked as he flipped a whole-wheat pancake.

"Mmm, smells good," Joanne muttered. "The concert? It was OK." Then she realized how she had sounded. "I mean, it was a lot of fun—"

"Well, which was it, OK or a lot of fun?"

Joanne went to the refrigerator and got herself a glass of orange juice. "The concert was fun."

"But?" Mr. Trask said. He lifted three perfect

pancakes off the griddle and placed them on a plate.

"But—" Joanne said. "But I'm feeling a little down. I'm not exactly sure why." She dropped dejectedly into one of the kitchen chairs.

"Here, take these." Mr. Trask put the plate in front of Joanne. "I was going to bring them to Grandma, but she can wait. It sounds like you've got something to get off your chest."

"You're right about that," Joanne said, pushing her long hair behind her ears. "I just wish I knew what it was."

"How about beginning by telling me how you felt at that concert last night?" Mr. Trask poured himself a cup of tea, brought some maple syrup to the table, and sat down across the table from his granddaughter.

"It was great. I definitely had a good time. But afterward, when we went to Rocco's, I felt, well, apart from the others. Sort of different, like I didn't really belong. You know what I mean?" Joanne dripped syrup onto her pancakes and took a bite.

"Sure I do. I think a lot of kids your age have those feelings. And you, Joanne, have even more reason to feel that way."

"I do? Why?" Joanne wanted to know.

"It's very simple. You're new here. Until recently, you hadn't even seen many of the things these kids have known all their lives. So much is new to you, so of course you'll feel a bit lost at times."

Joanne thought a moment, then took another bite. "You know, Grandpa, I don't think that's the problem. I do fine with the video games and rock concerts. I have a good sense of style, even though it's new to me. But I guess sometimes I don't care about all those things. I mean, I like them, but everyone else makes a much bigger deal about them than I do."

Mr. Trask took a piece of Joanne's pancake. "Aha! Now we're getting to the bottom of things. You have mixed feelings, Joanne, and that confuses you, especially when no one else seems to think the same way you do."

"Exactly," Joanne said excitedly. Suddenly she found herself pouring out an account of the conversation between her and Diane. "You see," she concluded, "they're all doing really interesting stuff on their own, but they don't talk about it, they don't—"

"Communicate?" her grandfather asked.

"Right." Joanne nodded. "So they get stuck doing the same things over and over. They're missing out on tons of fun together, just because they haven't taken the time to think of new stuff to do."

"And you don't want to be in that same rut?"

"That's it."

"Well, you've already done something about that. You asked Diane to take you to her ballet class. I bet the other kids will be just as willing to communicate and share if you approach them in the same way."

Joanne picked up her fork and played nervously with the food on her plate. "I guess so."

"But?" her grandfather said.

"But I wish my friends would be a little more open. I mean, I never would have found out about Diane's class if Rosa hadn't mentioned it."

"Hmmm," Mr. Trask said. "Joanne, if your friends haven't been open with you, maybe it's because you haven't been open with them. Is that possible?"

"You're really amazingly terrific."

"Well, I was sixteen once, too, you know. Now tell me what I said that was so amazing."

"You said I haven't been open. And you're right. I didn't even realize I wasn't showing my true feelings. Grandma told me before that I should try my hardest to be true to myself. Grandpa, I haven't been doing that. I was so busy trying to impress everyone that—"

"That you forgot to treat your friends as individuals," Mr. Trask finished the sentence for Joanne.

"Right. Oh, Grandpa, that was terrible of me. I

never would have done that to my friends in Scranton."

Mr. Trask took his granddaughter's hand silently and let her continue.

"I didn't try to find out what they were interested in, so they didn't tell me, and they didn't ask about me. I used them so that I wouldn't be lonely. I didn't share my inner thoughts at all. Why, Grandpa, I became as closed and tough as any of them."

"Well, dear," Mr. Trask said gently, "I don't think any great harm has been done. Those kids seem to like you very much. If you want to get closer to them, just open up, and I'm sure they'll respond."

"Well, I'm certainly going to try my hardest!" Joanne exclaimed.

Later as Joanne walked slowly toward Candle Garden, her sketchpad tucked under her arm, she thought back on the morning. What an incredible amount she'd learned. And her grandfather! Who could ask for anyone more understanding?

Now, as she wandered toward the park, she thought about some of the changes she wanted to make in her life. For one thing, she was going to spend more time doing just this—walking in pretty places and enjoying the outdoors. The mall was great, but not all the time. Then, she was going to try to be more open and giving to her friends, doing things with them one at a time so that she could get to know them better.

But most important, she wasn't going to put on any more acts. She was just going to be herself. If people didn't like that, she'd find other friends. But she had the feeling that Rusty's gang would like the real Joanne fine.

Then a horrible thought began to grow in Joanne's mind. What about Tony? True, he hadn't been very understanding about her problem with Skye. But she'd blown up at him like a real nut case. No wonder he'd stayed away from her after that.

Joanne thought long and hard about that as she walked. She really wanted to cry, but she held back her tears. If there was anyone she wanted a second chance with, it was Tony. But she knew she'd never get it. What was done was done.

Joanne let her troubled thoughts pass and tried to enjoy the afternoon. The sun drifted lazily between the clouds. Here and there were patches of blue sky. Joanne smiled to herself. Even when the weather here was bad, it was beautiful. If she were in Scranton right now, she'd probably be wearing three sweaters.

In Candle Garden the flowers blossomed purple, yellow, and red. Joanne spent half an hour looking at the different blooms and smelling their glorious fragrances. Then she sat down behind the hedge to do some drawing.

It was a pleasure to sketch purely for enjoyment instead of for class. It felt marvelous. There was no pressure to make the drawings work successfully, just the wonderful, familiar feeling of putting lines and colors on paper.

Joanne drew a few pictures of daisies and roses, then tried her hand at an overall view of the garden. It was a complicated scene, and Joanne worked on it for a long time. When she was finished, she realized she had done her best drawing in months.

Hey, she thought, *why is this so good when my football scenes are such disasters?* Well, she'd have to show the drawing to Ms. Statman. Maybe her teacher would have an answer.

Joanne gathered together her sketching materials, brushed the grass off her legs, and stood up to go. She walked around to the front of the hedge, then suddenly stopped short. Sitting nearby on one of the benches was Skye. Her head was bent, and her long blond hair covered part of her face.

Joanne wanted to dash out of the park. The two girls hadn't had any words for a while, but the memory of Skye's cruel words and her own response still stung.

No! Joanne stopped herself from sneaking out unnoticed. *No, you're not going to run away from this girl,* she told herself. *Skye has faults, just like you, and feelings, like you.*

Joanne walked up to Skye with determination. "Hello," she said in a friendly tone. "It sure is pretty here today."

Skye looked up sharply. For a moment Joanne thought the girl was going to come out with another nasty comment. But then her face changed. "Hi," she said warily.

"Skye," Joanne began, "I just wanted to apologize for the things I said to you in art class that day."

Skye's mouth dropped open in amazement. A friendly apology was the last thing she'd expected from Joanne. "Th-thanks," she stuttered. Then she was silent for a moment. "Why are you saying this?" she finally asked suspiciously.

Joanne sighed. "Because I really felt bad about the whole thing. I was wrong," Joanne said with conviction.

"Oh," Skye said, surprised at the strength of Joanne's words. "Well, I—I'm sorry, too," she said hesitantly. "I wasn't thinking about how you must have felt when I teased you so much.

I—I've had a lot of things on my mind lately, and I know I've been on edge."

"It's OK," Joanne answered, shifting the art materials in her hands.

"Hey, what have you been sketching?" Skye asked.

Joanne opened up her pad and showed Skye the flower and garden scenes.

"Wow," Skye said, visibly impressed. "These are really special."

"Thanks," Joanne replied modestly.

"I knew you were a good artist, but these are beautiful. You should show them to Ms. Statman. She'd appreciate them."

"I was thinking I'd do that," Joanne said. "So, tell me, how did you find this little hideaway garden? I thought it was my own secret place."

Skye laughed. "And I thought it was all mine. But it's big enough to share, don't you think?" She smiled warmly at Joanne.

"I sure do." Joanne felt wonderful. Skye had accepted her apology; she was even acting pleasant. Joanne still didn't know what had made Skye so nasty at first, but whatever bad feelings had been between them were gone.

"Well, it was nice talking to you," Skye said sincerely, getting up to leave. "And thanks for giving me a second chance," she added shyly. "I know I started us off in a really bad way."

"It was my pleasure," Joanne said, and she really meant it. She watched Skye's retreating figure and hoped she was on her way to making a new friend.

Chapter Fourteen

It was difficult for Joanne to see Tony in art class on Monday. She tried smiling at him, but his return smile was only halfhearted. After that, Joanne buried herself in her work, trying not to look at the handsome face across from her. The one time she glanced up, it was Skye who smiled at her, not Tony. *What a change,* Joanne thought, *from the first week of school when Tony was so friendly and Skye was doing everything she could to make me miserable.*

After class Joanne showed her drawing of the garden to Ms. Statman. "Joanne, this is a stunning piece," the teacher cried. "Look at these lines. They're beautiful! You have a wonderful, gentle touch."

Joanne smiled happily. "Thanks, Ms. Stat-

man, I'm glad you like it. But what I wanted t
ask you is, why do you think this drawing work
when the football scenes don't?"

"Hmmm." Ms. Statman thought. "Joanne,
have an idea. What were you used to drawin
back home?"

"A lot of landscapes, some still lifes, that sor
of stuff."

"And now you're trying to draw people activel
moving, right?"

"Yeah."

"So you're most comfortable drawing thing
that are standing still, not ones that are movin
It's going to take time to be able to handle th
new, moving subjects with the same ease as you
landscapes. In addition, drawing people is di
ferent from drawing objects. One thing yo
might try is to do a portrait of someone sittin
still. Or you could try a self-portrait using a mi
ror. That way you'll learn how to draw peopl
without having to deal with movement yet."

"All right," Joanne said. "I'll start tonight."

"You'll be OK," Ms. Statmen reassured her
"All you need is some more practice. Anc
Joanne, you should be very proud of this garde
sketch." Ms. Statman handed Joanne back he
drawing pad.

Ms. Statman's enthusiasm carried Joann
happily through the morning. She still had a lo

f experimenting to do, but she knew she'd get ome really good results if she just worked at it. *And I will work at it*, Joanne promised herself.

Joanne bounded into the cafeteria later that lay and quickly spotted Rusty and Diane alone t a table. She grabbed a sandwich and milk, aid, and hurried over to her friends. "I knew I'd ind you two gorgeous creatures in here stuffing our faces," she said, laughing.

Diane giggled. "If madame could see me with his pie, she'd have an absolute fit."

"Don't listen to her," Joanne said. "If you gain a couple of pounds, there's just more of you to lance with."

"Hey, why so happy today?" Rusty asked. You're smiling like a maniac."

"A compliment from my favorite teacher," Joanne said, unwrapping her sandwich. Between bites she explained what had happened n art that morning. "Ms. Statman really meant what she said, too," she finished. "I could tell by her face."

"That's great," said Rusty.

"Joanne," Diane said, "do you still want to ome see my ballet class?"

"Sure I do," Joanne replied, starting in on her milk.

"Great. I thought next Tuesday would be a good time. How does that sound?"

"Just fine. I'm really looking forward to it."

"Hey," Rusty complained. "What's all thi‍ about? And how come I wasn't invited?"

"Joanne's going to watch my ballet class. An‍ you weren't invited because you never asked you could come," Diane told her.

"Oh." Rusty sounded a little envious. "That's good idea, Joanne. I wonder why I never though‍ of it."

"You can come on a different day, Rusty‍ Diane offered.

"I'd like that," Rusty answered. Then sh‍ leaned forward eagerly. "Guess what! Jami‍ challenged Ralph Lipito to a video game contes‍ They're doing it today after school at the ma‍ You guys want to come? I thought I'd go ove‍ there and check it out."

Joanne laughed. "I think I'll leave Jamie t‍ you. Besides, there's something I want to do thi‍ afternoon." She told them she'd decided t‍ explore the little beach she'd seen on her firs‍ day in New Falls from the fish restaurant. Some‍ how, she'd never gotten around to taking‍ closer look at it.

"I'd be up for the arcade," Diane said.

"Great!" Rusty exclaimed. "I'll meet you a‍ your locker when school's out."

That afternoon as Joanne walked quietly o‍ the beach, she thought about Rusty and Jamie

It was too bad Rusty was cool around him. Jamie really seemed to like her, but she never gave him a chance to show it.

Joanne sighed happily. She was glad she'd decided to go to the beach that day. The video contest would have been fun, but she felt pretty wonderful being here alone. The sun, low on the horizon, turned the whole beach a soft, golden color. And the water took on a delicate pinkish hue. The sharp cry of a sea gull and the gentle slapping of the water against the shore were the only sounds she heard. It made her feel so calm, so relaxed.

She breathed deeply. The air smelled of fish and seawater. She walked down to the water's edge to search for some brightly colored stones or bits of shells. The cold water felt good against her bare feet and ankles.

Feeling a little silly, Joanne ran a few steps up on the beach, then jumped wildly into the air. She giggled out loud. What a wonderful feeling. She ran and jumped again, then came back to the water and trailed her feet in the wet sand, making patterns.

A few sea gulls flew gracefully past her, not bothered by her crazy behavior at all. "Hey, birds," she called to them, "want to see me make the greatest sand picture ever?"

Not waiting for an answer, she found a perfect

flat spot, close enough to the water for the sand to be wet but far enough from it so that the waves wouldn't wash her drawing away before she had finished. With a stick, she quickly drew a girl dancing. She wasn't a ballet dancer, like Diane, just someone having fun, the way Joanne had been when she was jumping.

Then, she scooped up a few handfuls of wet sand and added them to the picture to make it three dimensional. Soon Joanne was completely dirty. Her jeans were soaked, her hair had been blown into a mess, and there was sand all over her face. She didn't care. She was having a great time, playing like a toddler on the beach.

She stood over the sand sculpture, looking down. Suddenly it occurred to her that this artwork had the sense of movement Ms. Statman had been talking about earlier. It was a pity her teacher would never get to see it. "Well, dancing girl," Joanne said to the picture, "it's been nice knowing you. Too bad the waves will wash you away tonight."

As Joanne turned away and brushed back her loose hair, she saw someone sitting on a hill at the top of the beach watching her. The figure lifted a hand and waved to her. And Joanne recognized Tony.

Her first reaction was to clutch at her hair, trying to get it into some sort of decent shape.

Then, realizing how hopeless that was, she just shrugged and walked toward Tony, who was headed down the beach toward her. *Oh, well,* she thought. *He's already seen me acting like a fool in the sand. Messy hair can't possibly make things worse.*

"Hi, Joanne," Tony said.

"Hi." Joanne blushed.

"I've been watching you for half an hour. You sure looked like you were having fun."

"I—I was," Joanne answered shyly. "You happened to come upon me in one of my sillier moments.

"Joanne," Tony said sincerely, "I didn't happen upon you. I came here on purpose to find you. I asked Rusty where you'd be. She was very nice. I—I was wrong about her when I said she had a chip on her shoulder."

"You came here to find *me*?" Joanne asked incredulously. "Why?"

"Because I wanted to apologize to you. Oh, Joanne, I was so wrong that night at the Sea Shack. I thought about the whole incident, and I can't believe I really expected you to understand and forgive Skye after she'd been so mean."

"Well, I wish I had. And I especially wish I hadn't taken out my anger on you. That was really unfair of me."

Joanne and Tony just stood in silence for a

moment, their eyes saying more than they dared.

Finally Tony shook his head and laughed. "So now that we've both forgiven each other and we're friends again, do you mind if I take a look at what you were making? You were certainly absorbed in whatever it was."

How could Joanne refuse those beautiful green eyes? "It's just a sand sculpture," she said shyly. "But go ahead and take a look if you want to."

Tony and Joanne walked side by side to where the water was just beginning to lick the dancing girl's toes. Tony stood tall and handsome, scrutinizing the sculpture. "I've never seen anything like this," he marveled. "You know, Joanne, if we could pick this up, cart it back to school, and submit it for one of your art projects, I bet you'd get an A-plus."

"Huh-uh. Ms. Statman marks for effort, not results," Joanne said, but the compliment felt wonderful just the same. Tony liked what she'd done! And suddenly she didn't feel self-conscious with him in the least, not even with her messy hair.

"Well, I saw the effort that went into this. And believe me, you deserve an A-plus for it."

"Why?" Joanne asked with a giggle. "Because I

made a complete mess of myself?" She brushed grains of sand off the back of her pants.

"All artists get dirty," Tony answered, smiling. He gently wiped some sand from her cheek. "You were like a little kid for the half hour that you were working on this, Joanne. I don't think anything could have brought you out of the world you were busy creating right here. I tell you, that's the kind of total concentration professional artists have."

"I'll go down in history," Joanne said. "They'll say I was the best sand sculpture artist that ever lived. Of course, no one will ever see my work before the tides wash it away except for the birds."

"I've seen it," Tony said softly.

"True," Joanne considered. "Are you sure you're not a bird?" she asked, pretending to be serious.

"She's very beautiful," Tony said, indicating the shape in the sand. "She's so free, jumping all alone on the beach, as if she's thanking the whole world for just being there. She looks a lot like you."

Then tenderly he drew Joanne to him and kissed her. His touch was as gentle as the waves, as heartwarming as the setting sun.

Joanne sighed. Was this really happening to her, or was she dreaming it? She'd imagined this scene for so long. But now that it was actually occurring, it felt better than anything she'd ever imagined.

"Joanne," Tony whispered, "I never thought I'd see you like this."

"Like what?" Joanne leaned happily into his embrace.

"So free, so relaxed, so natural. At school you always seem worried about what other kids are thinking of you. Except at the very beginning. Then you were more the way you are now."

Joanne laughed. "Most of all, I was worried about what *you'd* think."

"Really?"

"Uh-huh." She paused. "So what do you think?"

Tony laughed. "I like what I see." He took her hand, and they began walking down the beach together. "I knew this beach was special," he said. "But I didn't know it was this special."

"I like it, too," Joanne agreed. "We don't have beaches like this back home, but it reminds me of there somehow. I guess it's the peace and quiet. It makes me feel so content, as if everything is right with the world."

"I know what you mean," Tony said. "That's why I come here so often."

"Drawing makes me feel that way, too. Sometimes I get so lost in my picture, I forget where I am."

Tony smiled. "I knew you felt like that, especially after seeing you today. But I could tell by watching you in art class, too."

"So you did watch me!" Joanne cried with delight. "I always tried to get you to smile, but you kept turning away whenever I caught your eye!"

Tony bit his lip nervously. "Well, I didn't get the impression that you'd want to get into a serious friendship with me, and I didn't want a shallow one with you. And then there was that thing with Skye—"

"I have to admit, I felt pretty bad about that," Joanne confessed.

"You did?" Tony sounded very happy to hear it.

"Yes. But I learned my lesson. I've got to do what *I* think is right, not what someone else tells me is right. Even if that someone happens to be my new best friend. I even apologized to Skye the other day, so I think things are OK now. We might even get to be friends, with time."

"Wow, that's a relief," Tony said. "I guess you know how mad it made me to see you putting her down."

Joanne hesitated, wondering how personal she could get with Tony. She decided to go for it.

After all, she'd already kissed him. "I wanted to ask you—just what kind of relationship *do* you have with Skye? I know she dates your brother, but you're awfully concerned about her."

Tony threw back his head and laughed. "So that's what was bothering you! The fact is, she and my brother are so close, she's almost like family. Let me explain why I'm so worried about her. Can you keep a secret?"

"You can trust me," Joanne said.

"Skye is going through a hard time right now. Her parents are getting divorced. So she's very fragile. And sometimes she lashes out at people without reason because she's so upset about what's going on at home. I know she was pretty hard on you at first. I just kept hoping you'd be more mature than she was."

So that was why Skye had looked so troubled in the garden. All the time Joanne had been envious of the beautiful girl, Skye had been absolutely miserable. It was strange how things sometimes turned out.

"I wasn't too mature, was I?" Joanne said mournfully.

"Well, you were going through your own troubles, moving to New Falls and being thrown into a new environment. I should have been more understanding of you, too." Tony squeezed Joanne's hand gently.

"I'm glad that's all in the past," said Joanne, squeezing back.

"Skye told me she was jealous of you. Did you know that?"

"Of me? You're kidding!" Joanne exclaimed. "What could I possibly have that Skye doesn't?"

"She's jealous of your talent as an artist. You have a gift, Joanne. Maybe that was one of the reasons Skye picked on you so much. You see, right now, she thinks she has nothing but her looks. I guess that has to do with the divorce, too. She's uncertain of herself, and she thought you seemed very secure."

"That's really funny," Joanne mused. "She thought I had self-confidence, and I thought she did. Well, I guess we both learned something from all this. People aren't always what they seem."

"Then there's no harm done," Tony said. "And now, there's something I've been wanting to ask you for a very long time. Joanne, would you like to have dinner with me Friday night?"

Joanne stared into Tony's green eyes. "Yes, I'd love to," she said simply.

Then they were in each other's arms, and this time the kiss was not quite so cautious. Joanne knew she'd remember it for the rest of her life.

Chapter Fifteen

"Joanne, your friend is here," Mrs. Trask called to her granddaughter at precisely eight o'clock Friday night.

Joanne quickly took one last look in the mirror, patted her hair, which was styled in a beautifully twisted chignon, and walked regally toward the living room.

Tony was standing in the doorway. He looked casual but elegant in black cotton pants, a maroon shirt, and a black sweater thrown around his shoulders.

"Grandma, Grandpa," Joanne said to her grandparents, "I want you to meet Tony Corda. He's a friend of mine from art class."

"Very pleased to meet you, Tony," said Mr. Trask, walking over to Tony and extending his hand.

Tony grasped it firmly. "It's nice to meet you, too. Joanne has told me a lot about both of you."

"Uh-oh. She didn't say anything bad, did she?" Mr. Trask asked.

"Grandpa," Joanne cried. "Of course not!"

Mrs. Trask came over to where the others were standing. "Well, Tony, we've heard a lot about you, too, and it's all been good."

Joanne blushed, but Tony's smile reassured her that there was no reason to feel embarrassed. She liked him, and he liked her. They both knew that already.

"Well, you two certainly have more exciting things to do than stand around gabbing with us," Mr. Trask said lightheartedly. "So get on your way. And don't be home too late."

"Have a good time," Mrs. Trask added, turning to leave the room with her husband.

When they were alone, Joanne smiled shyly at Tony. "I know you like me better in wet jeans and a sandy face, but I thought it would be all right to dress up just this once." She indicated the red cotton sun dress she and Rusty had bought the day before. It fit tightly at the waist, then fell into soft folds around her knees. Red leather pumps completed the outfit.

"Just keep on smiling like that, and I'll be happy," Tony said. He leaned over and kissed Joanne lightly on the cheek. "Come on," he said.

"We have just enough time to have dinner before the show."

"What show are we going to see?" Joanne asked curiously.

"It's not your usual kind of show," Tony remarked. "But don't ask me about it. I want it to be a surprise."

"I'm sure it'll be a beautiful one," Joanne said. She slipped her hand into Tony's as they left the house. Tony led Joanne to his car, and in a minute they were traveling down the highway. Tony put some romantic music on the tape deck. Joanne leaned back in her seat, enjoying Tony's nearness. She felt so comfortable with him, they didn't feel the need to say anything in order to communicate. They both appreciated silence, she realized.

Joanne thought about Rusty's reaction when she'd told her about the date. Besides being excited for her friend, Rusty had spent an entire hour trying to figure out what restaurant Tony would take her to for dinner. She'd named all the most glamorous, expensive places around New Falls. But Joanne had known it wouldn't be any of them. Someplace simple, she was sure, was more Tony's style.

Good old Rusty, Joanne thought, laughing to herself. She was finally softening up a bit on playing nonchalant with Jamie. During the big video game challenge, Rusty had gotten so excited that she'd forgotten to keep up her -don't-care attitude. Jamie could hardly ignore the wild redhead rooting for him in the front of the circle of spectators. And even though Rusty had slipped back into her old act after Jamie's victory, he had asked her for a date anyway. Joanne realized now that Rusty was afraid of getting hurt, of being rejected, and that was why she had acted like she didn't care. Joanne felt sure that once Rusty felt more comfortable with Jamie, things would work out between them.

The restaurant Tony had chosen was called the Country Gourmet, a short but pretty car ride away from New Falls. Decorated all in wood, with fresh flowers and candles on every table, it wasn't fancy. But it radiated a warm, homey feeling.

The menu featured fresh fish and vegetables, cooked in delicate, tasty sauces. She and Tony shared their orders so that they could sample both delicious dishes.

"Tony," Joanne said, "this place is perfect. Rusty kept telling me you'd take me to Regine's or something."

"I've been there. It's fancy, all right, but the food is heavy, and they keep the lights so dim you can barely see the person across the table."

"I'm glad we're here, then. Looking at you i
half the fun."

"Only half?"

"I'm sorry," Joanne said. "But this dynamit
food is definitely competition for you."

Tony got serious for a moment. "So tell m
about yourself, Joanne. There's a lot we don
know about each other."

"Where should I start?"

"At the beginning, of course."

"Well, when I was born, I was very, very small,
she said. "Do you want me to go back that far?

"How about telling me why you came to Nev
Falls in the first place? I'm sure it had to be mor
than a lucky coincidence that we met."

"The main reason I came was to get some an
experience," Joanne said. "And I've certainl
done that. But I've also had some very valuabl
life experiences. Life in Scranton is wonderful.
see that more and more every day. But it's lim
ited, too. After living there for sixteen years, nc
too much happens that's unexpected. Here ir
New Falls, I feel as though a whole sparklin
world is opening up for me."

"What's Scranton like?" Tony asked.

"Small, for one thing," she replied. "But beau
tiful, too." Then she launched into a detaile
account of life in Alaska. "You know," she sai
when she had finished, "it feels nice to tal

bout home. I think I've avoided the subject. I uess I figured that up-to-date people didn't ome from hick towns at the top of the world."

"A town at the top of the world," Tony epeated. "What a romantic idea. I'd like to do a rawing of that." Joanne was touched by Tony's entiment.

After some delicious homemade blueberry pie nd fresh mint tea, Joanne and Tony were ready o go. "A meal worth eating," Joanne said as she tood up.

"Now for your surprise," Tony whispered as he d her from the table.

He paid the bill, then bundled Joanne back nto the car. After about two miles on the main oad, Tony pulled onto a tiny side lane, which wisted and turned through the golden hills. It as certainly a beautiful drive, but Joanne egan to wonder exactly where they were going. Funny place for a theater," she commented.

"I told you, it's not that kind of show. Now rust me."

"I do, I do," Joanne told him. "I promise, no nore questions."

At last Tony pulled the car to a stop at the top f one of the hills. "This is it," he announced.

Joanne looked out into the empty country-ide. There were a few houses in the distance,

but nothing at all on the hill except one lone tree.
"This is it?"

"Uh-huh. Tonight is Bryant's shower."

Joanne looked at Tony in confusion.

"For heaven's sake, Joanne, it's a meteor show. You know, shooting stars? We had to come out here to get away from the town's lights. This way we'll see better."

"A meteor show?" Joanne said, breathing a sigh of relief. "Wow. Tony, for a moment I thought you had really lost it."

"It's going to be one of the prettiest nights of the year. I wanted to share it with you." He got two blankets from the car, spread one on the ground under the tree, and motioned for Joanne to sit down. Then he settled himself next to her and wrapped the second blanket around them. They sat, waiting for the stars to fall, snuggling together against the cool night breeze.

"There's one," Joanne cried suddenly, pointing into the sky.

"Quick, make a wish," Tony said.

"OK. I wish that—"

"Shh, not out loud, or it won't come true."

Joanne closed her eyes. *I wish*, she thought, *that I'll have many more evenings like this one with Tony*. "Done!" she cried, opening her eyes.

"There's another. And, by the way, I'm wish-

ng for the same thing you did." Joanne
laughed, and Tony joined her.

"Do you know about the northern lights?"
Joanne asked.

"No. Tell me about them," Tony said, snuggling a little closer.

"In Alaska you can sometimes see beautiful
colored lights in the sky at night. They look like
something out of a crazy dream, with all those
streamers and arches of color."

"What causes them?" Tony asked.

"I'm not sure, but I think it's some kind of elec-
trical phenomenon. It's also called the aurora
borealis."

"Wow. I bet that beats these little shooting
stars."

"Well, it's more dramatic, but this is just as
beautiful in its own way. Besides, I never saw the
northern lights with such good company."

Joanne and Tony sat silently, watching the
sky and waiting for meteors. Suddenly it was
raining lights. All over the sky, stars slid, then
disappeared. After about fifteen minutes the
heavy shower stopped, and within half an hour
the show was over completely.

Joanne turned to Tony and said, "When I was
younger, I was always sad when I saw a shooting
star because I thought a real star was dying. I

was so happy when I found out they were just rocks burning up in the earth's atmosphere."

"But think about where these rocks came from. They could be pieces of distant planets. Some strange alien might have walked on them."

"That's neat to wonder about," said Joanne.

"Well, do you think we should go? It's getting cool up here, and I don't want your grandparents to think I'm getting you home too late. I intend to be around a lot, so I want them to like me."

Joanne laughed. "I'd rather stay here awhile more, but you do have a point about my grandparents."

On the ride home they talked about less romantic things than stars and planets. They got on the subject of art, and Joanne told Tony about how well her garden drawing had turned out. "What I can't figure out," Joanne said, "is why I'm so good at drawing landscapes and so rotten at drawing people."

Tony thought for a moment. "You know, Joanne, I don't think you *are* rotten at drawing people."

"My football series really is rotten, believe me. I see it, and so does Ms. Statman."

"But she didn't see your dancing girl on the beach."

"Hmmm." Joanne looked thoughtful. "You're

right about that coming out really well." She laughed. "My dancing girl is back in the sea where she came from."

"Here's something to think about, Joanne. Maybe you're choosing the wrong subject to draw for that series."

"Then you think I should give up on the football game and go back to drawing landscapes? But I'm learning so much trying to put movement into my pictures."

"No, I don't think you should go back to landscapes. You *do* need to try something new. Joanne," Tony said gently, "how much do you really care about football?"

"Not too much," Joanne admitted.

"I figured that was the way you felt. After all, you saw your first game only a couple months ago. You couldn't have developed a lifelong love for it."

"I see," Joanne said. "I should be choosing subjects like—like Rusty cheering for Jamie or Diane dancing because I really care about them."

"That's it," Tony said. "You should draw things you like, not things you think everyone else will."

"Hmmm," Joanne mused. "You're saying I have to be true to myself in my artwork, just the way I'm learning to be true to myself when I'm with other people."

Tony smiled in the darkness. "You could put it that way," he said.

"Wow, Tony," Joanne cried, "what a brilliant insight! It's really going to help me. I have a few thoughts about my next project already."

Before they knew it, they were back at Joanne's house. Tony got out of the car and came around to open the door for Joanne. "A true gentleman," she remarked coyly. He put his arm around her shoulders, and they walked up the path to the house. At the door they turned slowly to face each other.

"It's been a wonderful evening, Joanne," Tony said quietly.

"For me, too," Joanne answered.

"When can we see each other again?"

"As soon as possible," Joanne replied.

"Great, is tomorrow morning too soon?" Tony asked.

"Breakfast at the mall?" Joanne suggested.

"Sounds perfect to me. And then I want to see you the next day and the day after that and the day after that."

Then he leaned over and kissed her. Or she kissed him. Later, when they recalled their first date, they were never quite sure which.